When Strangers Meet..

When Strangers Meet..

K Hari Kumar

Srishti
PUBLISHERS & DISTRIBUTORS

Srishti Publishers & Distributors
N-16, C. R. Park
New Delhi 110 019
editorial@srishtipublishers.com

First published by
Srishti Publishers & Distributors in 2013

Copyright © Hari Kumar K, 2013

Typeset by EGP at Srishti

"Coz nothing lasts forever... Even cold November rain..."
— *Guns N' Roses*

To my father...

Prologue

May 21, 2011
Somewhere in Southern India
03:15 AM

Everyone in the coupe was fast asleep, some men were dreaming lustily about the amusing middle-aged woman in the next coupe while others were simply asleep. All lights were switched off inside the compartment, the only source of illumination was the passing track lights outside. The bulky man sitting on the side berth rose and slowly walked towards the washbasin at the rear end of the compartment. He pressed the lid of the tap upwards. A stream of water poured down onto his hands and hit the metallic sink. With his right hand, he splashed some on his dried up face. He repeated this four times more until he felt his drowsiness fade away into the night's darkness. He released the lid and the flow of water stopped. He moved towards the door, pulled down the latch with his right hand. His muscles almost tilted the axis of the latch. The door unlocked and he pulled it backwards as he rested his bottom on the door that had opened behind him. He looked out, it was dark, the moon was hard to find among the school of dark clouds, but there was some whiteness at one spot that he recognized as an effort by the lunar marvel to peep out through the clouds that had gulped it.

As he dwelled upon the happenings of the past, both long

unforgotten ones and the more forgettable recent ones, he produced a cigarette from his pocket and placed the filtered end in his mouth. He screwed the lighter and there was a spark, which went off in a second, another try and this time the lighter produced a bright flame that did not extinguish. He brought his face closer to the flame, there was the earthy smell of tobacco catching the first flames and soon the cigarette was ready for consumption. He turned the lighter off and put it back in his pocket.

'What if *his* words came true?' He thought as he inhaled a few vapors of tobacco, 'Oh God! Please find a way out, I do not want him to die! O Lord of Tirumalai, help me!' He prayed.

He exhaled a weave of smoke into the atmosphere. He looked at the K engraved on the wrist of his right hand.

A tear fell from his eye.

As the Sampark Kranti Express passed over the river Krishna, his heart passed through a bridge that separated hope from fear. Dawn was still awaiting its final call before the night could shed every inch of its eerie darkness.

There was some hope in the darkness, the hope of a bright dawn waiting on the other side.

Moreover, all he needed was some more hope.

Part 1
The Runaway

1

May 20, 2011
City Center Mall, MG Road, Gurgaon
09:15 PM

The stout young boy wrangled his *Signature* jeans over his waist as he walked in the direction of the girl. She was vexed out of the posh discotheque. The girl wearing a prickly white top and slick denims pushed her way out. The boy overtook and stopped her by stepping in front her, blocking her way. He saw his handsome face in her light brown eyes. The soft patch of skin covering her cheeks was as smooth as peach and as fair as milk.

The girl turned her face away from him, he insisted upon getting her attention. He sprouted harshly, 'Hey! Hey! You! What do you think you are? Huh? Some kind of a teenage drama queen???'

'Get away!' the peach-skinned girl waded away.

'Oh! Do not give me that *do paisevala* attitude of yours! You had your time with me and you should be proud of that, no one else's gonna treat you that way!'

'Just let me go!' She insisted.

'Who's stopping you? Go! I will find more like you.'

'Oh then what are you waiting for?'

'Waiting for you to,' he came closer and weltered through clenched teeth, '*Fuck off.*'

The eyes of the girl got dewy, he stepped aside and she rushed out of the mall, crying.

'Fuck You! *Tania Malhotra* , I am gonna be very big! I do not need your advice! Try finding for yourself some henpecked boy who would listen to your *eenie-weenie* girl-talks! I am not that guy!' He rushed back into the crowded mall.

Another teenager woofed behind the boy, 'What are you trying to prove, Jai?'

Jai did not turn around, he spoke while he still looked at Tania fading into the crowd huffing outside the mall, 'Who cares about her? When I become a superstar, such girls would be willing to die just in order to get my autograph. Let her piss off!'

'Hey listen to me, man. Call her back, she's a nice girl, you will repent later!'

'Oh! *Fuck you* Anwar! If you are so concerned, why don't you go and make up with her? I got better things to do than repent over stale food.' Jai boasted angrily. Clearly, his ego had surfaced out of bounds.

Anwar's face displayed a patch of concern for his friend who had been outgrowing himself with frustration over the past few days. He placed his left hand on Jai's right shoulder and pitched in with a softer voice, 'Look, she just asked you to be careful about what you are gonna do. Sometimes you make stupid decisions and then end messing up everything. She wasn't wrong at all!'

Jai brushed off Anwar's hand from his shoulder. He started walking towards the exit and in a moment, he was outside the lavish City Center mall. As he stood facing the overtly swift MG Road, he pulled a cigarette out from his pocket and lit it with a Zippo lighter. Slowly he started puffing smoke in and out. Slowly, He disappeared into the commotion that was the crowd moving around him.

2

May 21, 2011
Prakash Bhawan, Gurgaon
10:15 AM

The atmosphere inside the Sharma household was red hot as usual. Prakash Sharma, the mathematics professor from Delhi University picked up whatever that was lying in front of him and threw it at the wiggling teenager standing at the corner of the dining room. Luckily for the young chap it was *just an onion*, unlike yesterday when he was hit by a storming night-torch!

He dodged the onion but before he could do it again, something else hit him on the forehead and it exploded. The pulp poured down his nose and streamed into his mouth. He yelled 'Dad! For the sake of your dumb God photos, stop throwing *onions* and *rotten tomatoes* at me!'

'Damn it son! How dare you enter my house at this time? Where were you last night?' The angry father screamed at his son.

'I...I was at Anwar's! We...were checking a few maths problems,' He knew the word *maths* could save a bundle of trouble, for his father could not be bribed with anything but the token of *numbers & equations*! Some anti-math students back in the university would joke about the Professor's marriage with the beautiful Mrs. Sharma. They would say that he married her just because she had the right co-ordinates at the right place!

'Oh! Now you think I am going to believe you. After all these years of studying maths at Anwar's you bring a *D* in maths and physics in your board exams! Are you even ashamed of yourself? Aren't you ashamed of lying to your father all the time?'

'But I got an A+ in English…'

'Shut up! I do not give a damn about it. Besides English is not even a subject. English is just a bloody language of people who ruled us like slaves for two centuries! But Mathematics is a universal truth! A real subject, a test of mental strength! It is the base of everything!'

'Then why do you teach maths in English?'

'Jai Prakash Sharma, you a think you are smart, little guy! You are not getting any allowance until you score a 70% in your first semester Mathematics.' Mr. Sharma declared.

Jai was shocked to hear the news, 'Whoa? Sem…sem…semester? I thought we were supposed to bite maths till twelfth only!'

'You got maths for 4 semesters in engineering colleges'

'*Engineering*? I mean, you are sick, dad! First you promise me that I have to deal with maths only till my 10th. After tenth, you tell me that it's just till 12th and now you say 2 more years!!! I mean 4 years, damn you, I am not getting into an engineering college, and I do not even have qualifying marks!'

'This is my house, I am the one earning here, and so, I call the shots here. You, my son, do as I say. Did you get me?' He pointed his fingers at his son.

Jai's face turned red with anger 'I hate you dad! You are the biggest liar I have ever seen in my life! Why don't you just kill me? I mean… It's better than studying engineering!'

'Shut up! And go to your room, get ready! We are going to Jagannath College of Engineering and you are coming with us!'

'But Dad, I wanna do animation! Learn acting side by side!'

'No more arguments. Get dressed in 5 minutes!' He ordered.

'I dun wanna do *engineering*'. Jai protested.

'Get dressed!'

Jai had no other option but go to his room and get dressed as ordered by his short-tempered father. He opened his closet and put on the worst pair of jeans he had, the one that was torn from the bottom, and a shaggy white jumper over his naked chest. He pushed his hair apart, made a mess of his long spunky locks and without looking into the mirror ran downstairs. His mother was locking the kitchen entrance, she did not turn around to look at his son's new look. She commanded softly 'Dad's waiting in the car, run along before his anger shatters the windshield.'

He walked slowly towards the steel colored *Maruti Alto* waiting outside his house. His mother locked the front door and followed Jai to the Alto. Both of them entered the vehicle together through the two rear doors, Jai from the left and Mrs. Sharma from the right one.

'You must be wearing that damn deodorant! What's that called?' Mr. Sharma thought for a moment, ran his retentive head for the brand that most of the Indian boys were addicted to, 'AXE! Yes, it's good that you are sitting in the backseat with your mother. I can't bear that killer smell! '

'Shut up! Dad, I do not use AXE, ok?' Jai argued.

'You new generation kids only know the ways to defy your parents. Argue with your father, do what they ask you not to do and that is your *dharma*!' Mr. Sharma's voice shifted its pitch from *mildly angry* to *I am going to throw you out of the car mode*. 'You people only want to dress up like film stars, flirt around with girls, and stuff! Back in our time, we would help our parents with all the domestic duties and still find time to study and excel in academics.'

Mrs. Sharma knew this was going to be another long filthy ride. She made an effort to end it before it would get worse. 'Prakash, stop it! Let him do what he wants to. He is much better than other kids his age.'

'You!' Mr. Sharma pointed at his wife, 'are the reason for all this! He is spoilt and useless, just because of you.'

'Hey Dad! Can you do us a little favor?' Jai insisted.

'What do you want now?'

'Just shut up and drive us to the hellhole you are taking me to.'

An emotion of red tanned anger ran over Mr. Prakash Sharma's pale face as he pushed the accelerator hard enough to set the road on fire.

'Hey! Slow down, you are gonna get us all killed! Are you crazy?' Jai shouted at his enraged father who was driving the car like a tainted emu.

What a life, what a father! Jai thought as he tried to keep his cool.

3

May 21, 2011
Ghittorni
11:15 am

On a very hazily lit noon, when one could see enough to distinguish darkness from light, the little boy turned his head first to his left and then to the other side. Then he checked straight, as if in a single stride he would measure the entire length that he was meaning to cross to get to the other side of the road. His destination was a dusty container office across the road that took care of the construction site booming in that part of the village. His father had told him 'Arshad, when you grow up this place will make you rich and we will open a bigger tea stall *outside* the mall so that more people can drink our tea.'

'What is a mall, Abbu?' he had asked innocently.

'It is a big shop that has everything in the world. You will like it.' His father had told him.

'Why can't we open a shop inside the mall?'

'We will do that too, we will do that. But you must serve very good tea to those good people who are building it. It is your job to make them happy.'

'Yes, Abbu!'

Now after a year of serving tea, he was familiar with almost everyone at the office. He believed his father was closer to their dream as well.

He felt dizzy, almost felt like dropping the gripped semi-dozen cup holder on the road and go into deep hibernation. A slumber that would last long till all his pain would go away. He wanted to go home. He looked up at the sun that poured its rays through the clouds and the scorching light hit his little face from a distance that seemed lesser than the distance between the spot he was standing and his home. He knew the sun was closer to him than his mud house because he could see the sun from where he was standing but his little mud home was nowhere in sight.

In a most unlikely manner, he started waddling across the highway. An Outlander was speeding towards him. He did not have the patience to look around again so he started crossing the road, unaware of the giant Japanese SUV. He took two more steps and that's when he noted that the bisonous monster was just a second away from crushing him to death. He stranded himself from taking another step, the outlander passed just millimeters off his toe and he could feel his soul almost reverberating off and back into his body. His heart pounded faster and the whole universe broke into a deafening silence. The clouds rumbled against each other and soon there were thunderous sounds of approaching rain. The thunder brought his life back to normal. He realized that he was very much alive and started his remaining journey across the road. He had life enough to reach the office, serve tea to the gentlemen and then wait outside on the torn cushion until they would call out his name. Occasionally he would be tipped by the generous supervisor. He would happily accept the one rupee coin as if it were some precious treasure.

He now stood on the divider, which meant he had crossed half the highway and had another half to cover. With another stroke of breath, he jostled through the remaining half and this time the journey was quicker. The tarred highway ended and a muddy track appeared, leading towards two containers with windows and a door. His face carried no smile, but a look of dismay.

There was no security guard at the gate or maybe he did not notice him in the haste. He moved quickly through the muddy track and in a minute, he was inside the office. Maybe the guard was calling out his name, but he did not care. He was too tired to stop by the old guard. He did not even knock on the door today.

He placed a cup of tea on each of the six tables for the officers. He had done his first task, now he had to wait outside on the cushion. He stepped outside the container and just next to the water-pot, he placed the cushion. The throne reserved for him. He rested his bottom calmly on the cushion. He was exhausted, almost dehydrated. He looked up: the sky was cloudier than it had been ten minutes ago. There were more sounds of thunder and as he looked at his wounded palms, a drop of water fell on them. Rain had started pouring. Unfortunately, it was both full of hope as well as dismay- the very sound of rain. He had prayed for rain when summer began, but the boon turned out to be a curse.

The rain would soothe his skin for the time being but few hours of continuous rain would wash away his mud house and he feared being homeless again. It was an arduous job to put the house back in shape. In the last downpour, the flood swept the house away along with his father's savings. He had heard his father tell his mother 'Allah had willed it this way. He must have better plans.' His father was always optimistic.

The rain was getting heavier, little Arshad pushed the cushion backwards and sealed himself under the tin roof.

He waited till they had finished with their tea and more importantly the chit chats over tea. Usually, he would listen to their conversation from outside. They would talk about various worldly matters and most of them passed over his little head, but he liked to listen nevertheless. But, today he simply sat there- Blank!

He wished he could also dance to the tune of the rain like other kids his age, like his brothers. But he knew he couldn't for he had responsibilities. He had to work hard for his brothers, for himself. Every rupee earned was a heartbeat added to their life.

He looked through the tinned roof and the raindrops. He kept staring.

4

May 21, 2011
Delhi-Jaipur National Highway
11:35 am

Jai peeped out of the window; he hated what he saw outside-RAIN!

There had been silence for a few minutes after they had stopped arguing. The brief strip of silence commenced the moment they had crossed the second tollbooth on the Delhi-Jaipur National Highway. Unlike the highway that passed through the New Gurgaon city where one could only see sparkling towers on the right and lush buildings on the other side, this was something he had never seen before. The highway was now running across the outskirts of the city, somewhere he had never been before in his life. He saw greenery on both sides of the highway, long strips of land that ploughed handsomely and heavy monsoon had caused outgrowth of green weeds. Though weeds, yet they were very pleasing to the eyes as the city boy continued capturing the beautiful sight in his mobile's camera. He could easily feel the fast-paced life retaliating down his bloodstream while a fresh stock of oxygen from the countryside rushed in to take its place.

He got his head back inside the car, turned towards his mother and spoke hesitantly, 'Mom, I got the forms from *Animationboxx*, they are giving a three year bachelor's in animation and multimedia.

I would like to apply for a scholarship too. In that case, I can study for no fee. All I have to do is give a written test and prepare a short animated film. The scheme closes in 3 days. But I need 1200 bucks for registration.'

Before she could reply or even bring about any expression on her pale face, the old man punched on the accelerator in great rage and in the span of a millisecond the car was zipping at a hundred and twenty kilometers per hour, on a wet road at a time nothing was visible through the windshield due to heavy downpour of rain.

'Could you please slow down, dear?' Mrs. Sharma requested her husband.

'SHUT UP! *Idiots*! Our house is a mess. You people are disgusting!' he yelled.

'Hey! Why don't you just kill us all? Huh?' Jai asked in disgust.

'Yes! That is exactly what I am going to do. After spending all these years working my life off for you people, all I get in return are sarcastic replies and an *E* in maths from my son! I will kill us all. *Bastard*!'

'*FYI*… *You* are the father of this *bastard*!' he nulled.

'Shut up!' Mr. Sharma pressed on the accelerator.

'Mom, what the hell did I say? I was at Anwar's, is there something wrong with that. Why can't he act his age?'

'You know your father. He is 52, but he is as immature as you are! At times, worse than you.' She shivered while replying.

'When will you learn to be disciplined? When I die?' Mr. Sharma enquired.

'Dad! Stop it; if you drive this way, you will never get a chance to see me disciplined! I will do whatever you want, just slow down!' He surrendered. Jai was trembling. He knew his father was a man of his word; so he apologized for the time being.

Mr. Sharma took his foot off the accelerator and squeezed

the brake, the car skidded across. A sigh of relief ran over Mrs. Sharma's face and Jai simply ignored what he had said a second ago and looked at the poverty-ridden kids *dancing in the rain*.

After a peaceful 30-minute ride in the car, they finally reached the destination – Jaganath Engineering College, a group of lackluster and forcefully western buildings placed at uneven distances from each other in an isolated campus. The air around the campus was of wet earth and the ambience was good enough to sweep any nature lover off his feet.

Mr. Sharma proudly announced 'Look at this building, don't you feel majestic that you are going to study in this blessed place for the coming four years of your life?'

Jai wished if he could kill his father and thereby serve his term in prison that would be better than studying maths, physics and shit like that for the next four years or *maybe more*! He did not bother to reply.

'Now come on, quickly, before they close down.' Mr. Sharma said impatiently.

5

May 21, 2011
Jaganath College of Engineering
12:00 noon

The dysfunctional family was inside the office building. There were three officials sitting at the reception. Mr. Sharma told them that they were here to meet the Chairman of the college. He showed an appointment card. The woman in the western outfit directed them to the Chairman's office. Jai could not take his eyes off the woman's shapely butt. He wished he could stay at the reception a little longer. The receptionist opened the door to the Chairman's office for the visitors. Jai was the last one to enter. Jai observed that the office was quite small and the illumination was very dull. He felt like choking. In one corner of the room lay a table with the nameplate that read 'R.K. Jain', the letters punched in gold lying reluctantly on the plate. The man sitting on the chair welcomed the parents and made them sit.

Mr. Sharma greeted the Chairman 'Good afternoon *Jainsaab*, I am Professor Prakash Sharma, Mr. Chillar must have ….'

'Oh Yes! Yes! Mr. Sharma, sure. Of course, how are you? You work at Ranjit's place.' The fat man exclaimed.

'No, I am a professor at the university, my wife works for Ranjitji.' Mr. Sharma corrected.

'Oh! Your wife must be badly qualified, I presume, for she works at Ranjit's place.' He remarked sarcastically.

'I'm a B.Com state rank holder.' Mrs. Sharma boasted.

'Oh! Still you are working at such a place. Must have done your bachelors' from a third rate institute. I wish our college were available for people like you. You would have reached the greatest heights...'

'We are not interested in my wife's masters'. We are here for our son's admission' Mr. Sharma interrupted.

Jai could easily notice the shift in his father's mood.

'Very well! How has your son fared in his 12ᵗʰ? The chairperson asked.

'I managed to pass.' Jai replied.

'He got a D. He scored pathetically in maths. It is my subject and that is why he does not like it. He hates maths and physics.' Mr. Sharma said. Jai tried to pass a forceful smile to hide the shame that his father had just filled in his mind.

The fatheaded Jain had managed to read the tensions in that family and fear in the father's mind. His cunning mind had already calculated a potential moneymaking scheme to fool this loosely bonded family.

'So, you want to be an engineer?' he asked as if he really cared about it.

'*My father* wants me to be an engineer.' Jai said frimly in strong words. He looked at his father, who was fuming from inside.

'Ok! I get it. Do not worry; our college will change your mind as soon as you get in here. We provide engineering in four streams- Computer Science, Information Technology, Electronics and Mechanical Engineering.' He elaborated.

'*Oooh!* I get to choose now?' Jai asked sarcastically.

'Hmm...very much!' Clearly the element of sarcasm had passed over the fat man's head.

Jai looked at his father, grinned a little and then asked, 'Which one has got the least *maths* in it? I will take that!'

'Information Technology has maths for 3 semesters, which is the least among the others.' Mr. Jain explained.

'Okay!'

'So, it is!' The chairman declared.

The chairman was a fat man with pale white skin and balding hairline. His eyes were wide but small as if they never opened more than a millimeter. He knew he could churn out as much money as he wanted from this pair of eager and anxious parents. They were worried about the future of their only son and would be ready to do anything to keep his future safe. Rather trust anyone who would just promise a safe future for their son.

He looked at Mr. Sharma and said, 'Since you are a mathematics professor, you must be well versed in numbers.' he chuckled, 'Let's talk about his capitation'.

'Well,' Prakash nodded.

'You know, I sold my last seat for IT at 6 lakh rupees, but since you are here on my friend's recommendation, I'd consider some relief for you.'

'6 lakh? But he told us 3 lakh!'

'Well, yes. But then you will have to settle for Mechanical and I do not mind it. But ask your son first!'

Jai's eyes opened wide in shock. '6 lakh for a seat in an engineering college. Just the admission fee! I could complete my entire course in animation and *acting* with that amount!' He *thought*. He looked at Mr. Jain who was asking him something.

'Would you like to opt for Mechanical Engineering?'

'No! It's IT or nothing!'

'See, Mr. Sharma, now you must decide if it's money or your son's satisfaction.' the academic merchant tried to bargain emotionally with the vulnerable distressed parent.

'Huh! Yea right, if he had cared so much for my satisfaction, he would have never brought me here in the first place.' Jai told himself.

'Sorry, did you just say something?' Jain asked Jai.

'No…No!'

'Okay, IT, how much for it?' Mrs. Sharma asked.

'Oh! Very Good, we could settle for three, I guess.' the businessman offered.

'Three? But we have got only 2.5 and we can't afford more.' She yielded.

'Oh! Sorry mam but I'm afraid I can't give your son that seat at 2.5 lakhs, especially with such low scores.' He replied dismally.

Bastard! 2.5 lakhs for a seat in an unknown college! You think we are fools? My parents may be, but I am not. My friend got in for free last week. Jai thought.

He wished if he could snatch the cup of tea the chairman was sipping and throw it straight on his fat face, *piping hot tea.*

'hmm…okay, since you have been recommended by Ranjit, I will relieve you off that 50 thousand.' Saying this, the fat man pressed a buzzer on his table and the sexy receptionist arrived once again with her beautiful bottom.

Damn! If I could only lay my hands around those. Save me!. Jai tried to pull back his mind off the receptionist's buttocks.

'Yes, Sir.' She asked.

'Provide these good people with an admission form and guide them through the rest of the procedure. Take them for a tour of the college. Make them feel comfortable.' He turned towards Mr. Sharma 'Have you brought the money with you?'

'No, I shall pay on Thursday'

'Oh! Okay, make it quick, I cannot guarantee you a seat if you are late. Our college is the most popular college this season'

'Yes, I will.' Mr. Sharma sighed as he gave Jai a demanding look.

Jai did not like even a bit of what was happening in that room. He wished that his father would turn down this offer and let him do what he wanted.

'Ok, Mr. Sharma, see you on Thursday' Mr. Jain said. It was his style of saying- *ok the deal is sealed. Now fuck off, do not waste my time.*

The receptionist led the visitors out of the room and took them on a brief tour of the college. Jai was no more interested in the events or the college. He was disgusted with his father and the bloody leech whom he had seen in the Chairman's room. They were looting foolish parents who were desperate. How could such a person ever find peace in life? Just a week ago, his former classmate, Rahul got a seat for himself in the very same college for free with a C in his exams. How much difference can *one* grade make? He wanted to tell his father about this, but he knew this was not the right time. He should stop his father from paying that lump sum of money. Thoughts ran in his mind from all possible directions.

It had started to rain again and the three rushed towards the car parked in a corner near the entrance.

6

May 21, 2011
Ghittorni
12:01 noon

The rain was pouring heavily on his naked body and the chill almost froze him to the spine. He felt as if he was being punished for the sin of being born. He carried the empty teacups in his right hand as he tried to cover his head with the left hand. He was rushing back to his father's tea stall. He had always worked hard for his father. His father had worked harder for his family and that was the one thing that kept little Arshad going. His biggest inspiration was his father. Every Friday evening, he and his father would walk to the town and purchase one weekly lottery ticket to test their luck. Many Fridays had passed since they started their routine of testing their fate. They would eagerly check the results in the Saturday newspaper for the previous week's draw. The little boy would wait for a joyous outburst from his father while he would go through the printed matter only to end up feeling disappointed yet hopeful for another Friday.

After walking for almost a mile, he could see his little village and the houses and among them his little tea-stall at a distance. It was normal to have five or six people waiting outside at this time of the day. However, today there were more than just six people. A herd of waggling people had gathered around his mud hut too. His heart thumped harder and before it could thump again, he heard a shriek from inside. He recognized it as his mother's voice. His heart almost popped out of its compartment. He feared that something had happened to his youngest brother who was suffering from some blood related ailment. On the other hand, could it be his father? Tears started filling inside his eyes. He prayed to *Allah*, just as his father had advised him sometime back. He knew *Allah* would solve all the problems of the determined and the hard working.

He was there, right in front of all the people standing outside his hut. He pushed through the group of anxious people. He entered the hut, he saw his brothers standing in front of the little kitchen, all four of them. He looked around, his mother was talking to Kasturba kaaki from the grocery store and she was in good shape too. He feared the worst, for he could not find his father around. He grew more anxious. Two or three more faces entered his hut and none of them was that of his father. His beady eyes started losing hope, a grim air of grief conquered his chest, and he wanted to burst out into tears. He controlled his grief. Sulked in a tear that was about to fall off his eye. Before he could ponder more, he felt himself separated from the floor below. Was he flying?

Someone was lifting him up from behind. The person turned young Arshad around and now he could see the person's face. Abbu. A smile came across Arshad's face.

'Son! Our problems are finally over! *Allah* has heard our prayers. He has gifted us heartily. We have won this week's jackpot!' The person exclaimed in joy. It was Arshad's father and he hugged his father with joy. The warmth passed from father to son and Arshad's frozen body was filled with life once again.

He placed his chin on his father's shoulder and looked outside, the rain was gone. He could see a spectrum through the door, A Rainbow!

7

May 21, 2011
Gurgaon
06:05 pm

Mr. Sharma was driving the vehicle at a very steady speed and this time Jai was sitting next to him on the front seat.

'Look, son, I am spending all my savings on your education, I have nothing else left with me for your mother and myself. You must start acting with maturity now. Forget everything that you did in the past and start over afresh now! Start a mature life, wear decent clothes, get an acceptable haircut and comb it like an engineer, like a professional!'

Jai's eyes searched for a way to begin his defense, '*Dear Dad!* I appreciate what you are trying to do for me.'

'You have to!' he demanded.

'No! You remember Rahul from my class?'

'Yes, I do.'

'Well, he got into the same college *for free!* That *fat ass* chairman guy is trying to misuse your innocence and desperation.'

'Watch your words, son!'

'Dad, he had a C, which is not much different from my D.'

'Do not tell me what to do. It's *my* hard earned money. You just study hard from now on.'

'But, Dad! Why can't you send me to a place where they teach animation? It will cost much lessr and I bet I can get that scholarship.'

'Shut up! You do not know anything about life. I did not sleep for 4 hours and teach a bunch of idiots for 15 years just to watch my son grow up and *draw cartoons!*'

'Dad, Animation is more than just *drawing cartoons!*'

'Oh Now, you are trying to *teach me*? You argue with me? *You son of a...*'

'Stop it! *You are my father*, stop swearing at your own son.' He looked towards his mother and said, 'Mom, how many times do I have to remind him?'

Mr. Sharma's temper had crossed all borders, and was now willing to blast off once again. He thumped down on the accelerator 'You do as I say. All my life I have worked my ass off so that I could give you everything that I did not have when I was your age and what do you give back in return??? *DEFIANCE!*' He shouted.

'Dad, I am not defying anything, I am just trying to pull you out off a scam! These people are just money minded rodents and I know the quality of the engineering colleges here, they are pathetic. Once you pay, their goodness is over! Besides, I know I cannot do this. Engineering is not my cup of tea.' Jai pleaded, there was that baffling expression of helplessness on his whitish face and grimly a tear dropped from his eye that sliced over his dark stubble.

Mr. Sharma shouted once again, this time almost forcing a tear or two from his red eyes 'You *Bastard*, I gave up everything for you, and you do not want to be an engineer for me? You do not want to listen to me. I am spending my money, why do you care. I am just asking you to study what I want. You filthy dog!'

'Mind your words, you are talking to your own son!' a timid Mrs. Sharma shouted ineffectively.

'Both of you are driving me crazy and I am going to end it now! You are all going to hell and guess who is taking you? *Me*!' The old professor once again pushed down the accelerator and the Maruti Alto slithered swiftly on the wet asphalt, luckily the road had very little traffic, almost none.

'Dad, stop it, you are scaring me!' Jai averted.

'I should have tamed a dog instead; at least it would have been loyal to me.'

'So, why don't you go ahead? I am sorry; I am not the tail-wagging dog you ordered!'

'Get out of my car!' Mr. Sharma pulled brakes and the tires almost burnt on the road.

Mrs. Sharma came back to life, all this while she had been frozen to death because of the speed with which her husband was driving the vehicle. The smell of burnt rubber tyres kissed her nose as she inhaled enough air to start her dose of *compromise* speech. She tried to bring the two to compromise, 'Son! Why don't you just shut up? We can talk about this at home. And Prakash,' she looked at her husband who was red as a brick that was containing some kind of an acid fume, 'please, control your anger. Drive slowly. Take us home. We can sit over tea and talk this out.'

The angry father started the car and drove at a considerably lower speed, they were heading home, and Jai knew this was it.

It was now or never.

The moment had come to make a final call.

8

May 21, 2011
Ansari Houselhold, Ghittorni
08:15 pm

Hussain Ansari and his wife Saira were preparing *Biryani* for dinner. The little kids were eagerly waiting for the delicacy for after a long time they would taste real cashew nuts. It was a joyous atmosphere at the Ansari household. Arshad, though, was sitting quietly near the window. He watched the moon as it tried to push through the clouds. The rain had stopped hours ago. He was happy that his hut wasn't washed away again. He looked outside through the window. He had never found the night so beautiful before. The creaking of crickets sounded less disturbing and more rhythmic.

'Arshad, dinner is ready, come here.' Hussain called his eldest son.

He ran to the dining area. His brothers banged on their plates while his father placed a big plate next to his. He called Arshad towards him. Arshad smiled and sat next to his father. The floor was cold, but the warmth of his father's love did not allow the cold to freeze his bottom. His mother brought the Biryani in a huge vessel and served it to the kids and finally to their father who were all waiting for the moment when they could pounce upon the delicious food, like hungry little cubs waiting to rip open the ribs of the deer preyed by the lion.

The dinner passed quite swiftly. After a long time, the kids and parents, both were going to sleep on a full stomach. Hussain stopped by Arshad's sleeping mattress. Arshad was almost about to sleep. Hussain kneeled down, ran his palm softly over Arshad's soft brown hair.

'Didn't I tell you Arshad, *Allah* pays everyone?' asked Hussain.

'Yes, Abbu.' Arshad nodded.

'Tomorrow I will be going to Delhi, I have got to sign few papers and then we will have our prize money in a few weeks' time.'

'What will we do with the money?'

'We will clear all our debts, build a pakka house in the town, cure little Latif and send all of you to school, so that you can grow up to become *engineers* and policemen.'

'But I do not want to study, I want to become a tea seller like you.' he replied innocently, after all his father was his greatest inspiration.

'Son, there is nothing in what I do.' The father replied with tears in his eyes, overwhelmed by his son's innocent love for him.

'Can't we buy a shop in the ma...*male?*'

'Ha ha', Hussain chuckled heartily, '*Mall,* son, it's called Mall. Yes, we will do that too. Now sleep well son, tomorrow you have to wake up early and run the tea stall in my absence. *ShAbba Khair* Arshad.'

'*ShAbba Khair* Abbu!'

The little boy dozed into the world of his dreams.

The overwhelmed father started walking to the room where his wife was waiting for a dose of blissful love. It had been long since the two had found time for love. The constantly recurring problems of life had always kept their love life on the backseat. But tonight, things were different, the burden over their heads were lifted off by a fate that looked promising hitherto.

A new day, a new life was awaiting them. They had hit a jackpot worth 50 lakh rupees. Time was money; they have enough money now so they have enough time too. Time to love, time to enjoy, time to live.

Saira closed the door from inside and soon the lights were turned off.

It was time to make love.

9

May 22, 2011
Prakash Bhawan, Gurgaon
00:00 midnight

Jai had had enough. He couldn't take it anymore. Sick and tired of his father's anger and dictatorship, Jai had decided to break the shackles and run away from home in pursuit of his dreams. He wanted to become an actor, which had been his dream for the past 15 years. The day he had seen *Shah Rukh Khan* in *Kabhi Alvida Na Kehna* he had decided what he wanted. He wanted to be an actor like SRK. He even secretly called himself RAJ!

He tore off a page from one of his old *maths* notebooks and started jotting down a note.

Dear Dad,

I know for the fact that I couldn't never really live up to your expectations and you couldn't be the proud father of an A grader. In spite of me telling you a hundred dozen times that I can't and I don't want to become an engineer, you still want to send me to an engineering college sacrificing everything that you have earned till now. I can't do this, I can't hurt you more. I can't let your investment go to waste because I know I can never be an engineer!

You see, the path of my dreams is running opposite to the

path of your expectations. So, it's either your expectations or my dreams and I have made my choice.

Please, don't waste your time tracking me down.

Your son,
Jai

He placed the note carefully on the dining table and placed the key of his motorbike over it. He took his cell phone with him, a few hundred rupees and a bag pack containing his underwear and other *essentials*.

Jai walked towards the door stealthily, opened it and stepped out of his house. Carefully he shut back the door from outside. He turned around, the street was deserted, just like in those zombie movies he had seen on *HBO*. Moonlight was shining behind the intense cloud cover, it was beautiful. He plugged in his ear phones. He pressed the play button and it was his favorite song *'Vindicated'* by *Dashboard Confessionals*. He started walking, into the night. He had to reach Iffco Chowk metro station before his parents could find out what had happened. Once, he reached there, he would wait for the first train to New Delhi Railway Station from where he would board a train to Mumbai. That was his plan. Immature as it sounded.

Mumbai, He thought, would make his dream of becoming an actor come true. He hurried through empty streets, it was windy outside and he felt the chill almost demagnetizing him from within his veins.

He could sense something following him, but he was sure, it wasn't a ghost because he did not believe in ghosts. Though, He did not plan in turning around and giving it a look, for that might prove his deep rooted belief wrong. He kept walking, briskly. The music in his ears kept him away from the world outside to some extent, but the next track gave him some shivers as the phone started playing *Annie Lenox's Love song for a vampire.*

He knew there was something or someone behind him. He could almost sense it. He did not want to turn around and he knew that it wasn't a ghost. He didn't believe in ghosts for he did not believe in God either and besides ghosts didn't lick people's feet. He stopped and turned around; a stray dog was licking his feet. He kicked it away. The dog waddled off in disappointment.

He continued walking briskly. *The metro station* was roughly 6 miles away and he would take another hour to reach there at this speed. He couldn't find any vehicle at 1 am in the morning.

The young boy walked into the darkness.

10

May 22, 2011
Ansari Houselhold, Ghittorni
05:04 am

The first rays of the sun had chirped in through the window into Hussain's room. Hussain opened his eyes to the light of dawn. He turned around to find the bare back of his wife lying next to him. He touched her back and smoothly tweeted his fingers over her warm soft body. The previous night's love had refilled him with vigor and zest. He knew he had a long day ahead. He had to catch the earliest train to New Delhi, so that he could catch up with the officials before they left. Everybody knew how particular the government officers were about *punctuality*: They arrived an hour late but left at least an hour before their scheduled exit time.

After a quick shower he hastily munched on the previous night's leftover Biryani. He looked at his wife, who was looking prettier than the night before. She noticed him looking at her and smiled. He smiled back, 'Let Arshad take care of the stall today, Qasim Baba says he has precious hands. They say he makes lovely tea!'

'I know. It's in his genes. He gets it from you.' she averred.

'Do take care of the money. After all, He's a kid; do not let anyone fool him.' The soon-to-be-rich man cautioned.

'You do not worry about a thing. Try reaching the Lottery

office in time; you know how opportunistic these Government officials are. They just want a reason to run away from duty.'

'I still cannot believe that after all these years, our prayers have been heard by *Allah*!' he pronounced.

Saira noticed that her husband's pupils were dilated with what looked like tears of joy of the present or those of sorrow from the past. She yielded another consoling smile on her moonlit face, 'Times change. *Allah rewrites fate of the determined.* We worked hard to make ends meet but never missed a prayer, never committed any bad deed and on top of everything never blamed *anyone* for the shortcomings but trusted *Allah*. This was *His* way of paying back. He always puts *His* children through tests, you passed them.'

'We passed them.' Hussain corrected his wife, '*Ya Allah!*' he raised his head to the skies in gratitude.

After finishing his breakfast, the tall man rushed into the bedroom, opened the *almirah* and pulled out a long white kurta. The white traditional kurta was given to him by his father on the occasion of Eid, six years ago. He kept it like a treasure in remembrance of his father who had passed away a week after that. It was already six in the morning, the first train left at 6:20 and it would take him exactly thirty minutes to reach Ghittorni Metro Station on foot. He was happy to see little Arshad already at the tea stall, setting up the kettle on the stove for early morning customers. Arshad saw his father looking at him. Arshad smiled and bid goodbye '*Khuda Haafiz*, Abbu!'

Hussain smiled back '*Khuda Haafiz*, Arshad!'

Hussain started taking in the air, he was excited yet there was some anxiety within him.

He had never dealt with so much money before.

As he walked, he passed by the huge under-construction site for the mall. The workers had started assembling at the site for the day's work. A supervisor was conducting morning attendance of the crew. He remembered his son's wish, '*Can't we buy a shop in the ma...male?'* he had said last night. A hearty grin appeared on his withered face. He tried to keep it as light as possible. But the harder he tried, the heavier it grew.

The thought of 50 lakh rupees gave him a shrill through the spine, the hair on his body grew erect as he felt a rush of blood whooping into his head.

Can't we buy a shop in the ma...male?

His son's words kept bouncing off the walls of his mind.

Thirty minutes later he was standing outside the Ghittorni Metro station. His feet that never ran out of power, were ready to go few extra miles without break today. He checked the huge digital clock.

06:35

He had missed the first train. The next train for *Jahangirpuri* was scheduled at 06:40. He had five minutes with him to catch that train. The ticket counter was almost as empty as the station. The woman at the counter slowly picked up the board that said *OPEN* and hung it loosely over the hanger. She yawned out the previous night's incomplete slumber and looked at the tall Pathan standing outside the counter, staring right into her eyes.

'Central Secretariat, one ticket, please.' he requested.

'That would be 28 rupees.' the woman replied in a half-hearted tone, still yawning through the interface.

Hussain produced 2 ten rupee notes and 4 coins of 2 rupees each and placed it on the counter's interface, 'There you go, twenty eight it is,' He passed a friendly smile.

The woman responded with a fake smile as she handed out a blue token. She did not have to try it, it came automatically to her face as she was used to doing that ever since she was posted at that counter.

Hussain collected the token and started walking towards the security check. There were three beautiful women from the North East besides him who were waiting for the security people to let them through. The chief security officer was saying something into his walkie-talkie. His conversation seemed serious and words like *derailed, rerouted* and *subject* were being used frequently.

Hussain was still standing under the electro-magnetic pass-through, waiting for the policeman to come and check his *sleeves*.

Finally he heard the words *OVER AND OUT* and noticed the policeman placing the black device back on the table behind him. He instructed a female cop to do something and then came towards Hussain.

'Sorry Sir, but we can't let you pass.'

Hussain was startled at the denial, 'But Sir, You haven't even checked me yet!' he defended himsely.

'Oh! It's not because of you. We can't let anyone up there for the time being. There has been an accident. Sorry, needs cleaning up. All yellow line trains have been postponed for the time being.'

'But I have to reach the Delhi by 10!'

'I'm sorry Sir!'

'Isn't there an alternative?'

'You know, there is only one route here. But I guess you can make it almost in time if you catch a bus to Connaught Place from the Bus Depot.'

'The bus depot is an hour away from here!'

'If you are on foot!' The policemen commented sarcastically.

'Yes Sir, I am!' Hussain replied incessantly. Hussain didn't notice the sarcasm in the Security officer's words.

Hussain turned around and started walking away towards the exit.

The policeman called him from behind, 'Sir, if you are going back, you must return the token at the counter and get your fare refunded, since you haven't used the token.'

Hussain looked at the blue token that he was holding in his right hand, then glanced at the policeman and smiled gratefully. It was worth twenty eight rupees.

Twenty eight rupees meant a lot to him. *He wasn't a millionaire yet.*

He turned around and went back to the policeman. The man on duty awaited the Pathan's question.

'How long do you think will it take for the service to restart?' Hussain enquired.

The policeman gave a little thought, and then picked up the walkie-talkie and there were some exchange of words. He returned to Hussain who was waiting for an answer expectantly, 'around 2 hours, they say, the lines will be re-opened by 8 am.'

'*Shukriya, Sahab*' Hussain thanked and started walking away from the policeman.

He looked at the round token. He decided not to return it. And instead of doing so, he would wait at the Resting area.

As he started walking towards the *RESTING AREA*, anxious thoughts began flooding in his mind.

What if I won't be able to make it today?

What if I reach, but late?

What if they decide to hand out the money to the next winning number?

What will I tell my wife, to Arshad?

Maybe it's another test of His, Ya Allah! He inferred.

He pushed the token into a small pocket on the left side of his Kurta near the chest. The Resting Area was right in front of him, just a door that separated him from the small extension of the metro building. He pulled the door open. The chamber was empty. A score of seats waited for tired asses to occupy them. It was as if the seats were calling out to Hussain, 'Hey! Bring your ass on me, I have got the most polished surface, you can see your face, style that unsettled strip of hair on your grumpy head, if want to!'

Hussain sat on the very first seat that he saw.

The other seats seemed to exclaim in envy 'Man! The first one always gets to seat the first ass!'

11

May 22, 2011
Iffco Chowk Metro Station, Gurgaon
06:01 am

Jai had commenced his journey to the metro station ten minutes ago. He had spent the night at the basement of MGS Plaza. The MGS Plaza was one of those *safe houses* where a handful of hooligans usually settled down at night during their drug transactions. The place also acted as their shelter on nights when police dogs were running after the stink on their ass. Jai had once contacted one of the hooligans, Pappu Rao, for some *desi stuff*. The relationship with the dealer was short lived as Tania had found out about his inadvertent habits, and she insisted that Jai on quitting weed for good and smoking for better. But he could never let go his urge to chunk high once in a while. He still was a heavy smoker.

It always worked- lady love's blackmail! But not in Jai's case.

Jai had slipped in three hundred rupee notes into Pappu's pocket for a few hour's hassle-free stay at the place till sunrise.

Now, as the sun was shining on his thick white face, he took out the sunglasses from his back pack and put it on. He looked at the sun, which was placing itself firmly on the northern sky, through the brown glasses that he was wearing now. The glare was not as harsh as it had been a moment ago.

From the road, he stepped onto the concrete staircase of the metro station. He ascended the stairs and set motion towards the ticket counter.

The station was already well crowded, after waiting for 15 minutes in the queue; it was finally Jai's turn at the counter.

He peeped into the counter and requested for a ticket for *Rajeev Chowk*.

'The Yellow Line has been closed down for two hours. Sorry for the inconvenience.' The lady at the counter offered.

'I just saw you handing tickets to the previous person.' he asked in a rude tone.

'Trains are up and running up till Ghittorni though.'

Jai thought for a moment. He had to make a choice. Either he could get out of the bustling station, catch a bus and thus go to New Delhi Railway Station or he could go to Ghittorni, get out and wait for the line to re-open, and then travel hitherto.

Getting out of the Station at this moment was unsafe, as his parents must have woken up by now and would be tracking their *runaway* son.

'Ghittorni.' he commanded into the box.

'That would be…'

'I do not care, keep the change and give me the ticket. Quick!' He said as he placed a 50 rupee note on her table.

'You seem to be in a hurry! Did you rob a bank?' she said while handing over the token.

'No, There's a bomb waiting to explode.' He looked into her brown eyes and plunged the next three words like a rocket from Antarctica, '*in my ass!*'

Jai propelled himself out of the area, briskly passed through the security and gushed upstairs towards the platform.

He boarded the first train that arrived at the platform and 15 minutes later, he was at Ghittorni.

He got out at Ghittorni.

He descended the stairs and moved out through the exit.

The weather outside had changed; he was surprised to notice the cloud cover. Fifteen minutes ago, the sun was shining on him and now, he couldn't find the big ball of fire anywhere.

He waited at the bus stop that was less than a mile from the station. He looked around, there were shops selling furniture and interior decoration items all around. Ghittorni was the center of such things. It was very early in the morning, the shops were tightly shut.

Twenty minutes passed. There was no sign of any bus or even an auto rickshaw. There was hardly any movement on the road. It was as if the entire region had been evacuated and no man lived there anymore. The feeling of zombie movies crept back again.

His phone rang; he wasn't shocked to see the number on the screen.

It was his father's!

He disconnected the incoming call. He dismantled the phone and removed the sim-card from the sim holder. In a swish of a second he broke the sim card into two pieces and threw them away.

'You can still track me with this shit!' He told himself as he looked at his Nokia handset, 'I do not need you either!' He threw away the handset too. He saw the mobile phone bounce off the green grassy ground where it landed and then hit a rock.

'How will you track me down now?' he smiled wickedly.

The phone was a gift from his father on his 17th birthday. It had happened just a year ago and it never felt any longer before. There was no remorse or any signs of grief, not even of minutest significance, on his glowing white face. He had lost nothing in the nothingness that he thought he had been living in.

The nothingness of that place had started to disgust him. He was tired of looking at the closed shops. Besides, he knew that he wasn't safe at that spot anymore since the police could track his position with that one last call. So, he decided to return to the station and wait there until the routes were cleared. The Police couldn't be quicker.

He started walking back to the metro station. It took him another fifteen minutes and finally embarked upon the station entrance.

Back inside the station he noted that besides him, there were only 3 security personnel and a yawning woman at the ticket counter inside the station. The security guy standing outside the corner room saw the young teenager, he conveyed, 'No trains till 9!', and then stepped aside to reveal the board hanging on the door behind him, 'You may wait here till then.'

RESTING AREA

He walked towards the room. It was time to rest.

12

May 22, 2011
Prakash Bhawan, Gurgaon
07:00 am

'I am sick of this rat!' the angry mathematics professor shouted, 'What does he think of himself? Huh? He leaves me a note?' He showed a piece of paper to his wife.

Mrs. Sharma took the paper from her husband and glanced through its contents. It was a letter from their son, Jai. He had written that he was running away from home to chase his dreams. She crumpled the piece of paper, held it in her fist, and started weeping. She alleged helplessly, 'Oh my God! What do we do now? I should call the police now!' She jumped towards the telephone and started dialing a number.

Her husband pressed his index finger on the disconnect button of the phone. He snatched the receiver from his wife and put it back on the console.

'Why should we call the police?' He asked.

'What do you mean? He has never been alone in his entire life! What if something terrible happens to him? He cannot survive such a harsh world alone, not yet!'

'Exactly!' Mr. Prakash expounded like an eager wolfman.

'What? I... I do not understand'

'He is a *weakling* at heart. He will not be able to survive. He will be back as soon as he runs out of money. He has no other option but to run away from *tough life*. Where can he go? He will come back here.' he grinned at his thought.

'You are impossible, Jai's Papa!' Most North Indian women would never call their husband by name. They would call them by suffixing the word father along with the name of the child. Thus, the lovely Mrs. Prakash addressed Mr. Prakash as Jai's *Papa*. That culture is slowly disappearing as most modern Indian wives have fancy pet names for their husbands.

'He doesn't have the courage to...' He defended himself.

'Well, pick up your mobile phone. You are going to dial his number, *now!*' She shouted.

'Okay! Okay! Give me a second, will you?'

Mr. Prakash quickly pulled his mobile out from his pajama pocket. He could not see the characters on the screen clearly since he was not wearing his spectacles.

'Wasn't he supposed to be on speed dial?' The angry wife queried.

'Oh yes!' He quickly pressed down the button that said *3* for a few seconds and then the call was made. It was ringing and it kept ringing. After few seconds of ringing, there was an answer. The old man instinctively pressed the phone into his ears.

'The number you have dialed is busy. Please try again later!' the voice said.

He redialed the number, but again the same answer popped up. This time it did not even bother to ring.

'He switched it off, I think!' He inferred.

'*Ram! Ram! Ye kya kardia tumne?* This is all your fault!' She started beating her fists on her breast.

'Shut Up! Stop doing that, nobody has died! Our dear son has had an emotional outburst. That's all. Once he finds that real life is much tougher and leaves you with very few choices, he will find his way back home. He does know the way back, doesn't he?'

'But we should inform the police, please!'

'Let us wait till noon. If he does not return, I will call the police and seek their help. I promise you.'

'But…'

'He is my son, *after all.* Trust me, I know him. He will be back soon.' The professor who was generally strict reassured her in a surprisingly mild tone.

She knew he was right; she had every reason to trust him. He had always been right. She wobbled towards him and he held her tightly in his arms. She felt safe and prayed that everything would be all right soon.

13

~

The air inside the Resting Area was quite damp owing to the weather outside, which he noticed had changed suddenly from sunny to cloudy.

He had been waiting inside for about half an hour now and his heart couldn't beat any faster. But he tried to control it. He took a deep breath, and then exhaled it slowly, breathed in again. He tried to slow down his heart. The third time he inhaled, the lone door opened suddenly, the activity took him by surprise and his breath was left hanging in mid air.

A young boy, fair and well built had entered the room. He looked around the empty room for a seat and then the boy saw Hussain. He stopped looking around and asked Hussain, 'When will the train for Jahangirpuri arrive?'

It did not take Hussain much thinking to answer such a simple question, for that's what exactly he been told a few minutes ago, 'In 2 hours.'

'Oh! Thanks.' He nodded and moved on to the last seat of the second row.

Although Hussain felt it very strange on the boy's part to sit in the opposite corner of the room when all the other seats in the interim were vacant, he did not want to think much about the boy's choice of seat. He had deduced from the boy's appearance and clothes that he belonged to an upper middle class family and could not be expected to talk to a poor tea stall owner like him.

Hussain thought about his own son, little Arshad. He was just six years old and was taking care of their little business in his absence, by the time he reached the age of this teenager who had just come into the room, Arshad would be married and still watching over the coiling tea kettles!

Can't we buy a shop in the ma...male?

Hussain chuckled to himself. With the fifty lakhs that he was about to receive, little Arshad's fate could be re-written. He could go to a school, a good one rather. Learn to read and write, get acquainted with numbers and study Science. He would learn how man had created this beautiful nation. He could find the answer to the question that he always used to ask, *'Abbu! How does milk become tea?'*

But for that to happen, he must reach the lottery office by 10 am. He feared missing out on the deadline. If he did, his dreams would be shattered. And for that very reason, he hadn't allowed himself to dream much more than what he had just thought. He had spent the night dreaming his wife's and thus saved himself from weaving a dream about all the things he'd do with the money. His wife, though poor, had the most beautiful body in the world.

Perfectly shaped!

He heard the door open again and seconds later there were some sounds. He didn't bother to look up. He felt the cold air brushing against him. For a moment, Hussain shivered. There was some form of movement from where the boy had seated himself. Hussain did not turn around, he tried to bring his stream of thoughts back to play mode. He heard him speak. It was the boy. Hussain turned around. He saw the boy who was speaking.

Hussain locked his view on the boy.

The boy noticed Hussain staring at him and did not feel comfortable at all.

He tried to ignore Hussain. He did it well and with ease.

Hussain had to choose the same option; he turned around and tried to get back to his own thoughts.

14

~

May 22, 2011
The Resting Area, Ghitorni Metro Station
5 minutes ago

Jai found the presence of another person in the same room uncomfortable. He wanted to be left alone for some time. So, he had chosen the seat in the further corner to stay away from real people no matter even if it was just one odd looking person sitting quietly, in another corner of the room.

He placed his bag on the seat next to his and opened the chain in its front section. He drew out a bottle of mineral water and started drinking from it.

He was putting the cap back on the bottle, when someone spoke to him.

'Excuse me? Can I sit here.' Asked the voice.

Jai looked up; he saw a body, over weight, of average height with a pot belly that could hold a dozen gallons of fat. His eyes travelled to his face, it was round and dark, darker than his arms. On forehead there was a vertical stroke of holy ash or *Vibhuti*. He was smiling broadly. The smile was powerful enough to shatter a glass made of diamond.

Jai gestured to his right; all the other seats were empty. He wanted to tell the guy 'Why do you not find yourself another seat, all of them are empty!', but before he could say that, the fat man reasoned, 'These seats are all dirty, it will spoil my westi'.

Jai had not noticed it yet. The fat man had said weste. The man was indeed wearing a westi. A length cloth that South Indian men drope round their waists to cover the lower part of their body. Here, in Delhi, they simply called it a *dhoti* or some ignorant people called it a it as *lungi*.

Jai was not in a mood to argue, so he picked up his bag and placed it on the floor, near his feet.

The fat man passed by Jai and then placed his huge ass on the next seat that seemed too small for the huge ass.

The strange Pathan had also started staring at Jai, which further irritated him.

What *are you looking at?* Jai shouted at the Pathan in his mind.

'My Name is Iyer, Krishnaprasad Iyer.' The fat man introduced himself as he held out his thick brown hand.

Jai took his eyes off the Pathan and looked at the fat man, he said in an irritated tone, 'So? Shall I get your name written on this seat?'

Iyer chuckled at Jai's anger, '*Ayyayo*,' he sighed in a very South Indian tone. He had a slight Tamilian accent to his English.

Jai noted that the Pathan who was staring at him was now startled to hear him talk to the stranger who called himself Iyer. Jai wanted to break Iyer's huge arms and smash the Pathan's head with that club of an arm! The Pathan turned around.

'What do you want? Do you know me?' Jai asked Iyer angrily.

'You know my name, and when you tell me your name, I will know it too. Isn't this how people *communicate?*' He paused expecting a reply from Jai. But Jai was not at all interested in Iyer's small talk, he tried to look away.

Iyer continued, 'You know, in Madras, they say…'

'I'm no *Madrasi* and nor am I interested in what people there say or how they say it. Do you get me?' Jai interjected Iyer.

'Your face is turning red, did you know that?' he said calmly, chuckling.

'Oh! So you read faces too?' he asked sarcastically.

'No, I was just *guessing*.' He chuckled with an extra stress on 's'.

'He He!' Jai imitated his laugh, the irritation clearly on his face.

Iyer ignored his irritation and continued, 'You know? Even I was once like you *vunly*,' he said only in a typical Tamilian accent, straight out of the streets of Madras. *Only* sounded like *vunly*. He continued, 'A *yangry* young man!' He paused to look at Jai.

'O Really? I'm really not int….' Jai was interrupted again.

'I had big dreams! Dreams that grew more and more out of reach and I also used to get frustrated like you. I would also talk to people like you- *yangrily*!'

Jai pretended as if he had not heard him. However, he did find some points that attracted his attention to Iyer's words.

I had big dreams! Dreams that grew more and more out of reach.

Iyer seemed determined to continue; he looked ahead and continued 'I used to quarrel a lot with my father! My house was more like a courtroom. Every word passed was an argument and every argument carried 440 Volts of electricity!'

Jai pictured his own life, the quarrels and verbal battles with his father. How they could never agree on anything. He peered at the Pathan sitting on the first seat. He wondered about the situation in the Pathan's house, if he had any.

Iyer continued his narration, he was still unaffected as to whether Jai heard him or not, 'My Father was a teacher at the Government School for boys. He wanted me to study hard and take up the same career!' Iyer chuckled.

Jai remarked 'Teacher?' It was the first time he had reacted reasonably to Iyer's narration.

'Yes, a very good teacher, in fact. And do you the funny part?'

'How would I know?' Jai retaliated.

The grin on Iyer's mouth grew wider as he spoke, 'I sucked in his own subject! And can you guess what his subject was?' Iyer paused but before Jai could even wonder, Iyer answered, 'Mathematics!' and started laughing loudly.

An expression of **Oh My God** grew on Jai's face. It was whiter than ever. It was as if Iyer was narrating the story of Jai's life. Iyer missed the changed expression on Jai's face as he was busy narrating his own story.

'You know he said that *the earth revolved around the sun and the universe revolved around Mathematics!* Something he learnt from an old movie. However, I hated maths. I could not even pass my matriculation exam because I failed in maths.'

'I can understand that. Man! Maths sucks!' Jai retorted.

'I felt the same way; I told you I was just like you.'

'Oh! Come on, Iyer! Just because we hate maths it doesn't make us similar. I mean, look at you! You are fat, ugly, wearing stupid clothes; look nothing less than a buffoon with that *thing* rubbed on your forehead. I mean, I am never gonna be like that.' He gripped his collar.

'Clothes do not make a person, dear. It's his beliefs!'

'Oh! Really?'

'You can bet, if you want to.'

'Ok! Listen, I am not interested in getting into any bet with you. I do not know you. So, would you please…'

Iyer interrupted him again, 'My name is Iyer, Krishnaprasad Iyer' He held out his right hand.

'Oh! Hell there you go, are you a moron or what?' Jai was vexed with Iyer's way introducing himself again.

Suddenly, the mysterious Pathan sitting on the first seat rose from his place and pushed out through the door. The room felt vacant and cold upon his departure. Was he also irritated by the fat Tamilian's presence in that suffocating chamber? Jai wanted to leave too, but decided against it. He was too lazy to leave. He had already walked many miles today and had slept in a basement parking lot of a mall! He wished Iyer would leave.

Jai bent forward, put his elbows over his knees, and rested his chin on his palms while looking down at the floor. He sighed.

'You still did not tell me your name, son!' Iyer remarked, 'I bet it is as beautiful as you are.'

'Why should you care? Are you some kinda South Indian homo?' Jai said without looking up.

'Oh! Come on. There is nothing wrong. You see, this is your problem. I think you are either too egoistic or too much of an introvert. Telling your name is not a daunting task. You should utter it with pride. A name is…'

'My name is *John Abraham*! Happy?' he almost spat out.

Iyer fell silent. For a moment, he saw the young boy staring at his face. This time, he did not miss the frustration in his eyes. The lines on his forehead were a clear sign of sleepless nights and stressful days.

After a minute of thinking Iyer reported, 'I think I have heard that name somewhere. Are you the son of some famous singer?'

HOLY CRAP! Is this man an idiot that he has not heard the Bollywood hunk's name or is he overtly sarcastic? Jai questioned his senses.

'My father is a darned professor.' Jai paused for a second, 'of *Mathematics!*'

'There you go! I know your name and a similarity between us.' Iyer smiled.

'Yea! Maths sucks! So, does my father.'

'Well, I thought just the way you did. I hated my father when I was 18. He would not let me do what I wanted to do. Always said that *Krishna, you will carry on where I left and grow up to be a maths professor* and I wanted to be an *actor.*'

Jai's eyes popped out. This had to be another coincidence and if it were one, then that would be too much to be counted as coincidence.

'You wanted to become an actor?' Jai queried perplexingly.

'Hahaha!' he chuckled, 'I know I am fat and ugly now, but I used to be fit and almost good looking back in my youth.' He surefooted, 'I had smaller male breasts!' The fat Tamilian winked and chuckled at his own joke.

Jai rechecked what he had just heard. He had actually heard the fat guy joke about his chest. The joke had struck Jai's funny bone. He chuckled heartily for the first time since last evening.

'I know it is funny. But my story isn't!'

'What's your story?' The words just poured out of Jai's mouth.

Oh shit! No, I did not say that! Revert it… Undo Undo! Jai's mind commanded but unfortunately his mouth had already signed on the agreement.

'Why don't we discuss it over a cup of *kappacheena*?' Iyer offered unassumingly.

'You mean, Cappuccino?'

'Yes, Yes!'

'Ok, I don't mind!'

Iyer produced two 50 rupee notes and handed it over to Jai, 'There is a Little Café outlet near the ticket counter. I will wait here.'

Jai was surprised, he felt idiotic, but had already taken the money from Iyer. He thought *what the hell! It's his money, I get free cappuccino.*

'Okay, will be back in a moment'

Iyer smiled as Jai ascended from his seat. He walked towards the door, pushed it and was out of the room.

15

Hussain was standing inside the telephone booth at the station holding a red colored receiver in his left hand. He waited until someone would finally pick his call and put an end to the continuous ringing.

The door of the temporary Resting Area opened and the teenager made his way out. The boy had two Fifty-rupee notes in his hand and walked in the direction of the booth. Soon, he passed the booth and swiveled towards the little café. Hussain watched the teenager running his eyes over the fancy menu displayed outside the cafe.

Jai ran his eyes from left to right, scanning the length of the menu displayed at the outlet. There were pictures of coffee in various flavors and styles. Then there were pastries and pasta, followed by his favorite- Truffle. The cappuccino was on the fat stranger. Just next to the cold coffee section was the list of available cappuccinos at the outlet. He ordered two regular ones at 49 rupees per cup. He placed his order at the counter, the guy immediately attended to him. He punched in a few keys on his keyboard, swiped on the screen once or twice, read the amount that appeared on the computer screen, 'That would be 98 rupees.' and passed a *customer friendly* smile.

Jai handed over the currency notes that Iyer had given him. The man at the counter collected it and placed it in the drawer. He tore out the bill that had appeared on the small printer and placed it in front of Jai along with a 2 rupee coin. Another employee of the Café brought two cups of cappuccino that were put on the counter, where Jai was standing. Jai picked up the cups and started walking back.

Hussain looked at the teenager. He had come in with two fifty rupee notes but was now carrying back a small coin and two cups of something. He knew it had to be tea or coffee but he did not know the mystery behind the disappearing currency. Just two cups of coffee churned out almost a hundred rupee from the customer! Hussain knew that people in the city were rich and things were costly, but there should be some limit. He would sell tea for 5 rupee per cup and coffee, which he made occasionally during heavy monsoon days and cold winters, would be sold for not more than 8 rupees. The coffee would be filled to the brim of the cup and the aroma would be enough to set the chilly weather on heavenly fire. Maybe his son was right; they should buy a tea stall in the mall. Nevertheless, he promised himself that he would not charge so much, so that even common people could afford them. But why was he carrying two cups?

'Hello, this is the Delhi Lottery Office.' The phone was finally answered; Hussain had shortly forgotten that he was waiting for someone to pick his call. His prayer was answered.

'This is Hussain Ansari, from Ghitorni. I wanted to know till what time the Superintendent would be available today.'

'He is here till 11.' The voice replied. It was a male voice and the accent was sluggishly Haryanvi. *Maybe Rohtak!* Hussain guessed.

'Oh, ok. Thank You. Khuda Haafiz' Hussain greeted and put the receiver back.

Hussain opened the glass door and went out of the phone booth.

Perhaps, I should consider my son's opinion, he told himself as he took long strides to the Resting Area.

16

Here's your cappuccino.' Jai handed over the hot cup of beverage to Iyer. Iyer threw his right hand around the cup. Jai noticed the tattoo '*K*' imprinted on his wrist.

'K? Are you from the same group as Karan Johar and Ekta Kapoor?' Jai enquired with a tinted sense of humor.

'No, No! It is the first letter my name. Krishnaprasad , K'

'Oh! Of course.'

'Sit down now, I have a story to tell. This doesn't even smell anything close to *Madras Kaapi*.' He complained sniffing the steaming cup of cappuccino.

Jai sat down on the seat next to Iyer; he noticed that there was some girl's name and number scribbled on the seat.

Shabhnam Singh – 91837218.

Attempts had been made to cross out the last two digits erased with a blade or something, though the curve of one of the two digits was still visible beneath the marks made by the blade.

Assholes! He thought.

As he sat down he asked Iyer, 'You love telling stories, it seems.'

'Do you know which is the greatest epic till date?' Iyer asked in an unassumingly degenerate way. He sipped from the cup in his hand.

'I am not into fantasy kinda shit.' Jai replied crudely.

'Come on! *Guess da*!' Iyer took a firmer grip on the boy's imagination.

'What? Is it Greek? Or wait…*Mahabharat*? Isn't it?'

'No! My dear. It's something that's more contemporary and realistic.'

'What? World War 2? Assassination of Hitler?'

Iyer chuckled, 'Hitler committed suicide. Try something personal.'

'Oh! Please, I am not into reading either. Would you please throw some light before I lose interest in your story?' He queried.

'It's your own life story.'

'I'm sorry, What did you say?'

'The greatest epic is your own life's story. From the moment you set foot outside your mother's womb, an epic was set into motion that will keep evolving until the day you leave this place. For some, the story never ends, their legacy continues.'

Jai was expecting a wacky answer from Iyer, but this came as a shocker. An artfully woven piece of philosophy from the fat man left Jai staring blankly at Iyer's face.

'Your *cappachina*…it is getting *cold da*. Drink it.' Iyer juggled between moods.

Jai picked up the coffee mug and started sipping the lukewarm beverage. He started liking the way Iyer would solder the final verb with the Tamil extension '*da*', it felt warm and awkwardly attractive. He did not know what it meant, curiosity to know the meaning made Jai ask his next question, 'Why is it that you keep adding *da* to every other verb? What does it mean?'

'something like *yaar* in Tamil slang.' Iyer explained.

'Yeah! right. So Can we start with the story?'

'Yes Of course, dear.'

Iyer inholed deeply, his fleshy chest almost expanded to the extent of blowing up the station. Then he let the air out, holding his lips in the shape of the English alphabet '*O*'.

He then narrated his story.

Part 2
Iyer's Story

17

May 1993
Pattabiraaman Kalyanamandapam,
Madurai, Tamil Nadu

Fresh out of Class tenth, Raamasaamy Iyer's son was the talk of the *Agrahaaram*! Nobody had written me off, but neither had any one ever expected much out of me. All the relatives from my *Agrahaaram* had complete faith in my cousin, Kamakshi and hoped that she would score the highest aggregate among us *equals*!

However, it turned out that she secured 94 percentage marks in her 10th class boards, which was two percentages lower than mine. Thus, I became the hero now.

Even I was little surprised at first. I knew I had done well, but so well? I could never even imagine in my wildest dreams that I could score over eighty percent! Maybe the examiner was either drowsy or too high while he was checking my paper or maybe it was checked by his two year old! Whatever the reason might have been, I was damn excited! Things were certainly going to change!

Kamakshi's father, that is, my uncle would often mock my Appa that I wouldn't score more than 60 in his subject, Mathematics! But to everyone's, especially my Appa's, surprise, I scored a whooping 99 out of 100! Happens! I was on cloud nine!

At least I thought so. Very confident of my life in future, I swelled up with pride. But little did I know that it was going to be the beginning of a lifetime of misery and discontent.

Here I was, attending the marriage of my mother's elder sister's second daughter's brother in law in a community marriage hall in Madurai near the Meenaksi Temple. Although, conceived at my mother's place in Madurai, I moved to Tuticorin with my parents when I was just a year old and since then I have been here. Never had the need to move out of Tuticorin!

Everyone from the *Agrahaaram* was present at the wedding. Oh! By the way, *Agrahaaram* is the term used for a street consisting of a group of houses, where most of the residents are related to each other. *Agrahaaram* derives from the two words *Grah* and *Haaram*. *Grih* is the Sanskrit word for house while *haaram* means garland. Thus, *Agrahaaram* actually translates into *Garland of houses*. It is a traditional system in southern India, especially Tamil Nadu where houses run parallel and meet at a temple. Well, not exactly parallel. Just try to imagine, I am not good at geometry, you will know that soon.

So, the houses actually bind the temple like a garland. The houses are inhabited by Brahmins and well, we were Brahmins too, **Iyers!**

And *My name is Iyer, Krishnaprasad Iyer*!

18

I was with my second cousin whom everybody called Kanna, owing to his dark mischievous face that resembled Lord Krishna's. The two of us got along pretty well, our aunts would often envy the bond shared by us and would try to create differences between our mothers to break this bond. Even if they were successful in creating difference between our *Ammas*, their intentions could never touch us. So strong was our love for each other. We would do everything together, talk to each other for hours without stopping. We never got bored when we were with each other. However, the thing that we liked most was, hitting on girls our age and elder to us especially at weddings and other such social gatherings. We would drape ourselves with whitest white of *mundu* and silk shirts and with our aviators on our faces; we looked nothing short of a Rajni and Kamal duo. I always preferred Rajinikant, although he was dark but he would be happy as Kamal. Being the taller and elder among the two, enjoyed a greater following and garnered more respect from the younger lot. There were 18 direct cousins out of whom, 15 were younger to me, while the three who were elder had been married off years ago. Therefore, I enjoyed a special status among the equals. So here we were, at the wedding of Ranganatha Iyer and Krishnaveni, eve hunting inside the wedding hall, while keeping our faces hidden from our dear parents. I was walking along the circumference of the inner sanctum when Kanna called me from the book, 'Thalaiva! Look at this. Sooooper-figures, Thalaiva!'

I looked around, 'Where *da*?'

Kanna was right behind me, and I saw him pointing his little fingers at two young girls clad in traditional *pattu pavadai*. *Pattu* means silk and *paavadai* means the lower gown or long frocks that run up to the ankle. Typical Tamil beauties, I thought.

'*Dei!* Slow down, too old for you,' I shot down my cousin, 'follow me.'

Kanna silently followed me; he knew I was in command there. He would call me Thalaiva, just like everyone else. Thalaiva means the leader of the herd. I was the leader of cousins and my friends. I posed a threat to all my rivals. Nobody rebelled against me at school either. I was the hero for everyone and now I was the hero for my family too after having scored a whopping 96 percentage. I was indeed Thalaivar! By the way, they also called me Thalaiva because I was a huge fan of Rajinikant, who is the Thalaivar of the world of Tamil cinema.

We passed a few grown ups and finally arrived near that door where the two girls were standing. One of them was dark skinned, fat nosed and not attractive while the girl with her was fair and gorgeous. The fairer one caught my attention and I really wanted to sweep her off the floor and carry her away from there. She had a beautiful and innocent face that matched the sweetness of *Sreedevi*, the greatest female actor. It was as if Goddess Lakshmi had herself descended on the earth. The long dark thick hair touched the floor while her carbon black eyes sparkled under the glow of camphor wavering in front of her. As I inched towards her, I could feel my heart pounding even faster than it was pounding a week ago, while Karuppu's German shepherd was chasing me.

How would I start it, the conversation? Should it be a preplanned dialogue from one of Thalaivar's romantic movie or should it be spontaneous and original.

I was just a soul away from her, before anyone could notice; I swished my aviator glasses back on my eyes. In a moment's invigoration, I pulled the trigger to my mouth, '*Vanakkam*! Girls' I said.

The two girls replied by staring at us, rather at me.

Kanna posed to fit into the contraption, 'This is Thalaivar, this year's 10th board topper. Thalaivar is our topper.' He could never be better; He knew exactly what would impress any South Indian girl or her parents and said the holy words 'Topper'.

The expressions on the girls' face changed. From hostility they were now those of incessantly ardent admiration.

'My name is Iyer, Krishnaprasad Iyer,' I threw the red carpet, then glanced at Kanna 'and that is my cousin Hariprasad', well yes, Kanna's real name was Hariprasad Iyer. The girls looked at one another, trying to convince each one to introduce her first. Finally, the darker one, whom I wasn't not interested in rolled out, 'I am Kaveri. I am the bride's niece.'

Did I really care about that? I was only interested in knowing the fairer girl's name and other significant details. I tried to look through her, well I had been staring at her since the moment Kanna had pointed them out to me. That was my style, never forget to give away the fact that you are indeed looking at a girl because you are interested in her. It always worked. Therefore, I kept on staring at her, almost drooling into the honey-like sweetness of her golden face.

She kept looking at me and when she noticed that I was looking at her, she looked at the floor. After a few seconds, she again looked at me to see if I was still looking at her, and again she looked at the floor for I had not taken my eyes off her. The fluctuation of the eyes continued for a moment that seemed far more than just a few minutes. Meanwhile, I forgot that the other girl, Kaveri was still introducing herself. I got back to her, she was still explaining, now in a bit more friendly tone, 'and I like to sing *Keerthanams* and perform *Bharathanatyam*…' My God! She had not completed yet. I had to stop her, 'Oh Fascinating!' I forced a smile on my face, turned back to the other girl, the fairer one! Did I miss her name, had Kaveri mentioned her name while I was in that deep trance? Whatever! I had to take my chance now, this was so much different from other weddings, from the other girls we had met, more specifically, and maybe this was her!

The girl from my dreams.

The girl of my dreams.

'I forgot, what was your name again?' I asked.

Kaveri tried to reply, but I pushed my right arm signaling her to stop. The other girl must have trembled. Yes, indeed she did. She attempted to open her lips and let the sweetest of *Thirumadhurams* ooze out in the form of words. The lower lip tenderly sliced out from the intersection it shared with the upper lip and the sound of bilabial friction almost shook my whole world.

'Pa...' I could only hear that much, just the first syllable of her name when I heard something terrible roar out my name.

'*KRISHNA*!'

That was my father's voice; the hungry lion must be looking for a prey to pounce on. Oh my God! Had he caught me hitting on young girls? Before I could answer, I felt a thump on my back, I turned around slowly. There he was... standing tall and broad like a mammoth. I am sorry I referred to him as a lion two sentences ago, but 'mammoth' is a much more appropriate word to describe his physique and 'lion' for his command over all of us.

'Yes, Appa.' I recoiled. We, Tamilians, address our fathers as *Appa*. That is the word for father in Tamil, *Appa*.

'What are you doing?' he asked suspiciously.

'Nothing...I..I.' *Goddamn!* I could not think of an excuse, 'Kanna and I here were...'

'Kanna? Where is he? He is not here.' Appa shouted, well, that was his normal mode of speech: yell!

I looked around; Kanna was nowhere in sight. Damn! *Naayi*!

'These girls here, Appa, did you meet them? They are the bride's relatives, very close ones.'

'So?' He moved his palm up towards his moustache. The thick brushy moustache! Unlike our other relatives who kept a clean shave, Appa loved to keep a thick bushy moustache.

'So, they were lost. I was helping them find their mother.' Finally, I made up something gullible, hoping it would work on my father.

'hmm…' He nodded, 'See, I told you Mr.Venkatachalam that my son is a gem! He is not just a topper but also smart and helpful. He is an all rounder.'

Mr.Venkatachalam was a fellow teacher at my father's school, who also happened to have a 15-year-old, studying in class nine. Maybe, it was Appa's way of telling everyone; hey, my son is the best. Appa moved closer and stood next to me, he placed his thick dark hands on my back and once again, the impact made an ear shattering sound. He smiled heartily and said, 'My son is an all rounder, an all rounder!', and as he smiled, I tried to force a smile on my face too. However, deep within myself, I was sighing in and out. The girls behind me were giggling; I could hear it, though I did not have the courage to turn around. Their giggles and murmuring were fading out; maybe they were slipping into the crowd.

In the far corner, near the sanctum, I spotted Kanna. He was peeping out of the sanctum. I grimaced angrily; he understood that he was going to receive a heavy dose from me later.

19

Mr.Venkatachalam was also smiling; he asked me, 'What's your plan now? What next?'

I wanted to say I was interested in films and wished to look forward to a career in acting, but before I could open my mouth, somebody else filled in for me, 'He is going to be professor of *Mathematics!* Just like his Appa. No.! Better than his Appa. Isn't it son?' He looked into my eyes and they bore deep into my emotions. For the second's sake, the question was addressed to me. Why was he answering it? Moreover, did he even know what I wanted? Mathematics? No way! Somehow I struggled hard to find a way out of it and again he was going to push me back into it! I wanted to rebel. Nevertheless, something deep inside asked me to be patient and requested me to stay silent.

However, little did I know then, the price I would be paying for that brief moment of silence.

20

Two years later, May 1995
Roach Beach, Tuticorin, Tamil Nadu
Early morning…

I walked on the shores of the Bay of Bengal with a cheeky teenager who was constantly looking at the glowing cigarette in my mouth. Finally, he asked, '*Thalaiva*! Give me one puff. Just one.'

I passed the cigarette.

He quickly took a deep puff and felt the concoction of tobacco smoke mixing up with the moisture on the walls of his throat as it travelled down his windpipe,

'Aah!' The short boy exclaimed as he exhaled a cloud of scintillating smoke, his dark eyes projecting the reflection of glowing cigarette in his mouth.

I peered into the waves on my left, felt a deep urge inside to express the innermost of my heart. I looked at the cheeky teenager who was still counting stars that the puff of cigarette just showed him.

'You know, Kanna, my results will be out tomorrow.'

He did not reply. He took in another puff from the cigarette. It seemed as if he had not heard me.

'I am talking to you, Kanna!' I agitated.

'Thalaiva, I know that too. Why worry about it? You are the best of the best, the All-rounder. You are our Thalaiva.' He replied. I was a greater fan of Thalaivar Rajinikant now. He had all the Tamil youth falling head over heels over his enigmatic aura. Thalaiva could do anything! Anyone who had watched movies of Rajinikant knew that. We were no different from other Tamil fans; both of us were huge fans of Rajinikant and were totally mesmerized by his character in Baasha, just like any other teenager in Tamil Nadu that year.

'I think...I think I will fail in maths!' I vomited those words. The sentence was followed by a grave stretch of silence. The expression on Kanna's face almost resembled that of a bombed Hiroshima.

'What?' He croaked after coming back to his senses. He dropped the cigarette from his hand accidentally, 'Shit! You have wasted my cigarette also!'

'I do not know. I could not do it! Maths is not my subject *da*.' I tried to explain.

'Exactly! It is your *Appa's* subject! Your father is a great mathematician!' Kanna shouted.

'I tried my level best, I did ok in the algebra questions, but trigonometry is going to cost me a year!' I confessed.

'But you said that you had done well, right after you came out of the examination hall, didn't you?'

'Yes! I lied. I was afraid of Appa's reaction had I told him that I did not even touch trigonometry while preparing for the paper.'

Kanna was shocked to hear that, 'You did not even cover Trigonometry, but why would you leave it? How many marks was Trigonometry worth?'

'40.' I shied.

'40? Out of 100?' he burst out.

'I am afraid so!'

'What were you thinking? How could you even pass like this?'

'I do not know. I just couldn't get any hold of it!'

'And you did not ask Appa? He is an expert in trigonometry.'

'It's not that, I just can't do it. I do not want to do it! That's it!' I declared.

'Do you know what will happen tomorrow? I mean, if you fail?'

I stopped walking, turned towards the blistering Bay of Bengal, gazed at the rising tides, 'I am leaving this place. I have my dream with me, the dream of becoming an *actor. The next Thalaivar of Tamil cinema.'* I paused to take in a deep breath of fresh air coming from the blue waters at the cost of the bay's distress, 'Madras is calling me. I feel it. If I stay here, I will go crazy under Appa's strictness. Have you seen this place? It's like a rotting jail!' I erupted. I looked at Kanna; he was not very shocked at this for he always knew about my craze for cinema and Rajinikant.

He did not say anything.

I continued, 'My dreams run in the direction of uncertainty and mystery. While my Appa's expectations run in the opposite direction. I cannot travel both ways. It's either my way or his.'

Kanna finally spoke, 'so, it is your way, I guess?'

I nodded 'Hmmm…'

He had tears in his eyes, 'What if the results are out, and luck brings a twist in your tale? What if you pass by luck?'

'I do not know what to do! I want to tell Appa that I do not want to study maths anymore. I want to join a film school.'

'What if he doesn't agree? Which I am sure, he would not.' he said.

'Then I guess I will have to make my own way.'

Kanna hugged me tightly as he burst into tears, 'I will miss you *Thalaiva.* I wish you all the luck and I am sure, in a few years, I will be watching the first day first show of your film. I will be the first one to stand up in ovation and shout your name out loud by in obeisance and celebration.'

There were tears in my eyes too, because it was difficult to let go of the things that made me, things that defined my very existence. Kanna was one of them and so was this coastal town! I will surely miss them. However, success demands sacrifice. All great men had given up their greatest pleasures to achieve greater success. *What am I then?*

'I will talk to Appa tonight, once we are back from Anita akka's wedding. Let him be free.'

'Amma and I are not attending the wedding because she feels that our religion will be corrupted by attending her wedding.' Kanna revealed sadly.

'She's afraid that you might find inspiration in Anita's love story and find a lover like she did.' I tried to lighten the mood.

But that wasn't enough to cheer him up. He knew things were about to take a steep turn and they would never be the same again.

Never again.

21

These two years after class tenth examination were nothing less than fantastic on a personal level, as I discovered my inner self, the passion I had in life. I realized that I wanted to be an actor. I went on to do many stage plays at school level and everybody knew that I was the best actor in Tuticorin. However, on the domestic front, things could not get any worse. My father did not like the very idea of me doing plays; neither did he embrace the fact that my academic performance was dipping an all time low owing to my participation in extra-curricular activities. Of course, he would not, especially when my cousin Kamakshi, whom I had *beat* by a couple of numbers back in tenth, was getting a scholarship in the United Kingdom.

It was the age when boys grew arrogant and were eager to argue with their fathers just to prove their view was the right one, while fathers would not give up their age-old conventional thinking even if they knew they were wrong. It was a matter of our respective egos. This happened at my place as well; there was too much tension between Appa and me. I had started publically displaying my dislike of mathematics publicly, which further aggravated my Appa's anger. After all, I was the son of an ardent mathematician!

I never lost a chance to mock the validity of mathematics in front of others neither did Appa leave out any chance to insult my ill-concerned attitude towards academics. In almost every social function that took place in the neighborhood or far and near family, Appa and I would get into some kind of a verbal duel which would go on to become the highlight of the event. People who were attending these events would often forget that there was a wedding going on somewhere under the same roof. Such is the lure of petty family fights. No wonder *Mahabharata* had such huge following.

With just a day left for the announcement of my board exam results I was sure I would fail in mathematics and might just manage to pass by one or two marks in Physics. Deep inside I wanted to tell Appa about my concern regarding the results, but I was afraid to do so. As always, I was afraid to confront *Appa*. Men grew sane with age, but this particular man had grown horns, red-hot horns straight out of hell.

If I told him that I had no interest in Science and mathematics or in becoming a mathematics professor; he would throw me out of his house. Furthermore, if I told him that I wanted to be an actor; he would shoot me with that rusty old gun that had been hanging on our wall for decades. Either way, I knew that soon, I would have to bid farewell to the paternal bonds that had been keeping me under the blanket until now. However, it was going to be sooner than I had expected. In fact, the trigger was about to be pressed in a short while.

The occasion had been the wedding of my youngest aunt, Anita Saarangam. Well, she will not be called Saarangam anymore, not after she got married. This was not like all the other weddings that had taken place in our family. This one was quite a treat for us youngsters while it shocked the elders. The reason: my aunt was the first person from our entire lineage of orthodox Brahmins to get past the shackles of Traditional *arranged marriages*. She had successfully persuaded her parents to allow her to marry her lover, who by the way was a Muslim – Imtiaz.

However, she was not the first one to be involved in a love affair, but yes, she was the first one to get married to her much coveted boyfriend. This event aroused great anger and was a matter of argument and disregard among all the elders. For three or four months after the matter leaked out, the entire family condemned Anita for crossing the line and her parents were blamed for giving too much freedom to her just because she was their only daughter. Her father was a man with modern outlook. Despite being abandoned by everyone, he never stopped counting on his daughter. He knew she was wise enough to find a good man for herself. After almost three months of hanging the decision in mid air, finally, my great *paatti,* that is, my grandmother gave her approval. God knows what had got into her at that moment when she approved of the marriage. I wished she would be equally generous with all of us too (just in case). Imtiaz's family agreed to the match on the condition that their wedding would follow pure Islamic traditions. Eventually, everyone agreed. They had to. So, here I was at Anita maami's wedding, a Muslim wedding, something to which I wasn't accustomed to.

I was excited because there were lots of new faces and unfamiliar customs. Some of them were beautiful and others wore long beards, while some looked just like my relatives. I was not interested in the bearded men. But strangely enough, I wasn't eve chasing either. Perhaps the fear of failing in mathematics had withheld the Casanova in me from getting out of his enactment area.

I peeped into the huge unroofed chamber; the cooking area. The smell was quite different from what we usually got to eat at our Brahmin weddings. This one had a tint of garlic and warm seasoned oils. The picture of Salim's Biryani showed up in front of my eyes. Salim was a classmate of mine who would often bring Mutton Biryani to school, and secretly I would steal his lunchbox and feast on his mutton chops. I loved them, but alas! I could not do it more often or in public for I was a brahmin! Condemned to grass roots and leaves! But never had I imagined I would smell so much of Biryani over Sambhar and rasam. I entered the room, and there were a dozen vessels.

I pulled aside the lid that covered one of the vessels; hot steam that smelled like clove oil in cashew stew brushed through my face. I breathed in the aroma, wait, there was more. The smell was followed by the sight of golden rice and pieces of mutton chops lying strewn here and there in between chunks of onion strips and broken cashew nuts. It was the turn of my mouth now to churn out every single drop of water inside my body and collect it around greedy gums, ready to drop out the moment I would open my mouth. I could not control my hunger, pride, or whatever. Just like I did back in school, I killed the Brahmin inside me (once again) and put my right hand into the vessel, pulled out the best-looking piece of mutton and pounced on it like a hungry wolf that had not seen food for a lifetime.

'*Krishna! Aiyayayooo!!!*' somebody called out from behind me, I knew somebody had seen me digging into the *unholy* vessel. However, the tone and the voice were both unfamiliar. The tone was not one that of anger or shock, but one that was jeering. While the voice, I knew did not belong to anyone from the close family, but I knew that voice. I was not able to recollect the owner of that voice, but I was sure that I had heard it somewhere before, maybe in a previous life? It was too sweet to forget.

I turned around, I saw a girl standing at the doorstep, pinning her right hand on the frame of the door and resting the palm of the left hand on her implicitly curved hip. Her brows moved in an interrogatory rhythm, twice; up and then down. As if asking, *what are you doing here?*

The eyes were, jet black like those of the deer. I was surprised, pleasantly surprised to see her for I never knew If I would be ever meet her again. Last time, I had seen her at a *close* relative's wedding in 1993. Her eyes had struck a deal with mine at that very instant when I had seen her. But sadly, my great Appa had interfered and I lost her, I couldn't even get to hear her name! All I had with me was the first syllable of her name '*PA*' and the visual memory of her *Srideviness*.

Now, after two years, here she was, standing in front of me while I, well, I had a piece of *unholy* mutton hanging from the corner of my mouth. I unsnarled my incisors and let go of the piece; it fell on the floor. I giggled in embarrassment, 'I thought it was a vegetarian... err...vegetable' I stammered, trying to hide the embarrassment.

'*Ahahaha!*' she teased in a typical Tamilian tone, 'Of course, it smells like drumstick, right?'

I chuckled.

'What else do you think besides considering me stupid? Eh? *THALAIVA*?'

She remembered my nickname, which brought out a spirit of romance within me. I struck back, like a young Romeo trying to impress his Juliet for the first time, 'I think....'

'What do you think?'

'I think that .... You are the most beautiful girl on earth.'

She started walking towards me, her eyes shimmered as the fire lighting the vessels behind me found a reflected image on them. There was literally fire in her eyes, and I could feel the heat of desire punching me in the guts. As she drew closer, I started trembling; I found it difficult to find words to spill out when she would start talking. She stopped, winked wickedly.

'It's ok, I am not telling anyone! Just get out of here before anyone else sees you.' She added.

'I do not think anyone from our families would come anywhere around here.' I shot back confidently.

'Oh! Really? Then what are we doing here?'

'I couldn't resist the luring smell, so I dragged myself in, to taste some Biryani,' I saw her smile at my reply, but my curiosity was expressed in a query, 'But what are *you* doing here? Were you too lured in by the smell of Biryani?' I winked back at her.

She giggled and replied, 'I saw a very familiar face sneaking in. Out of curiosity I followed that face.'

'Whose face was that?'

She smirked at my question and turned around.

I followed her, 'I'm sorry, wasn't I supposed to ask that?'

'Can we get out of this room please?' She pleaded in a commanding tone, a tone that I had started to like. First the biryani and now the girl who had caught hold of my fantasies since our first meeting.

Was I in love?

We walked out of the room quickly; I pressed my question again, 'Whom were you following?'

She gave me that look once again; I felt the *sreedeviness* in her again. Oh! I loved it.

'Are you acting stupid so that I can feel smarter?'

'No! Tell me, I was the only one sneaking into that room. But I do not think you would be so curious as to follow me, that's why I asked if there was someone else.'

'Unfortunately, I was following you.' She noted the tilt formed above my brow, 'Shocked?'

'Why?' I so much wanted to smile like a hopeless romantic, but I had to be a man here, so just came up with an innocent *why*.

'I remembered seeing you at that wedding in Madurai, two years ago. It was almost at this time, May or June.' She tried to recollect.

I was very happy to hear that from her, if I had my way, I would have lifted her by the waist and spun her around in a circle, just as they did in movies. The adrenaline had reached the joints of my fingers; they almost rubbed against each other in excitement. I tried my best to keep it plain and simple, 'Yes! Of course, now I remember you. You were with another girl.'

'Yes, that was Kaveri.'

'Of course, you know, we meet so many people every day that it is simply impossible to remember each one.' I made the most ironic statement of my life at that time, for here was the face I was looking for ever since that first meeting. Even she must have noted that, I started with a line, which sounded more stupid than flirtatious.

She kept staring at the mild brown spot on my white cotton shirt. The spot was the result of something that had happened while I was pouncing on the mutton biryani.

'So, are you planning to top the exams this time too?' She asked.

I didn't reply.

'You do not seem excited!'

'It's a long story!' I sighed.

'We have the entire afternoon, I guess.'

'I hope so….' I was interrupted by a demonic invocation.

'Krishna,' the demonic voice called out, a voice that I recognized very well.

I wished he could have interrupted a little later. After a wait of two long years, I finally had a chance to talk to the girl of my dreams.

'Krishna, are you deaf?' The voice asked again.

'Yes Appa, what is it?' I replied, I noticed that the girl slipped out of sight silently. I wanted to hit my head against the wall. I had missed her again. I had forgotten to ask her name, and I knew I would not be in a mood to look for the beautiful girl once I had met with my old man. This frustrated me, even before he had started talking.

'Mr. Venakatachalam wants to ask you something.'

Everything seemed to repeat itself, the girl, the same questions from people, high on expectations and now Mr. Venakatachalam. I did not care to study his face carefully, for I could still see that girl every where in my mind's eye. There was this killing frustration that constantly overpowered me. My father's friend was saying something; I did not hear as my mind was preoccupied.

'Krishna, did you hear what he said?' asked my father, the words from that voice would never miss my ears. Although they always wished they could.

'Yes!' I nodded without knowing what my father's friend had said.

'So, you have decided to study higher mathematics at the same place where your father was once declared the best student?'

That was the bomb, which shook my world. Although I knew my father wanted me to graduate in mathematics, he had never taken a final stand on that. I thought he would let me do what I wanted. He had even decided the college where I would be studying what *he wanted* me to study. To study what I hated the most- mathematics.

I stared hard into my father's eyes. His eyes were made of stone, thick black gravel that had no place for compassion or room for tolerance. The frustration inside me grew stronger and my face started turning red along with my eyes. Appa noted the change. He was agitated by the way I was responding to the situation. He hated the way I had learned to look boldly into his eyes every time we started arguing. He tried to suppress everything by pretending to smile.

Finally I spoke, 'I think it's high time. We have to talk about this.'

The words were directed at my Appa who now tried to ignore my question. He turned around and started greeting the first person who came his way.

I drifted towards him, called out 'Appa! I want to talk to you, now!' He ignored me.

I tried calling him again, but it was no use.

Then I tapped on his shoulder thrice, 'Appa! I know you are

trying to ignore me.' He said something, but it was too low for me to hear.

I could only hold my frustration to an extent. I broke out and with my hand pulled him around. The gesture moved him and rocked him like a piece of jigsaw puzzle falling out of piece.

Now, we stood there, face to face.

Man to man.

Father to son.

Son to father.

22

'How dare you use your force on your father?' He asked like Hitler in a dhoti, 'Have you forgoten your manners?' I felt him tremble as he said that, or was it the air around me that was quevering in front of the volcano that was about to erupt in few minutes.

'I just want to make a few things…clear!' I stressed each word individually.

'I do not have time for this.'

'Neither do I.' I pressed, 'I do not have time to follow your dictatorship.'

'How dare you say that?' He burst out with anger.

'I stand by what I said.' I replied. My reply irritated him even more.

'Now, you have started to mock your father's words. Have you grown older to me?'

'Yes, I have! For God's sake, I am eighteen years old and can take my own decisions. Let alone decisions, have you ever considered tending out what I think? At least, on matters that have to do with *my* future?' I paused to breathe, 'Look! I do not care what you want to do with your life or any other person's life. But, I can't let you decide what is right for me.'

'You are just a kid! You do not know anything.' Appa declared.

'Yes! I do not know anything, I do not know what you know, and do not know Mathematics! However, I know what I want to be, I know my passion. I know that I want to be an actor. And I know I *will* become an actor!' I declared.

'*Dei*! You are out of your senses!'

'No, Appa! Now I have come to my senses!'

Now, my replies were a decibel or ten louder than my father's statements and people had started gathering around us, but nobody tried to stop either of us. They wanted a fight; they were getting one that would be enough for the day's entertainment and would last for a month's gossip. Amma had also entered the scene; she was the first person who tried to stop me from continuing the argument.

'Why should I not say anything? Just now, this, Venakatachalam comes and tells me what I am going to do after my class twelve. He tells me which college I am going to join and what profession I have to take up! He tells me what *you have* decided for me. Then why do you even need me to be alive? You need a puppet, whose strings are always in your hands.' I inched closer to Appa, bore into his eyes, 'I am not your.....puppet!'

'Get this *stray dog* out of my sight or I will kill him.' My father commanded his brothers.

Without even a second's delay, my uncles surrounded me like goons from a Tamil movie. I bet many among the *spectators* expected a father-son fistfight, rather prayed for it to happen.

'I am not a stray dog!' I shouted and this time, my uproar almost stopped the wedding proceedings. Nobody except the bride, groom and a few person were at the proceedings, while everybody else was witnessing our heated exchange. I continued, 'I am tired of being your dog. Ever since I remember, I have been doing what you have wanted me to. I had never let you down. Now it is time I started making my decisions, this being first one that I make for myself. I can't let you dictate me throughout my life!'

'Krishna, leave it son, we can talk at home.' My Amma tried to bring down the temperature, but it was of no use.

'Amma, leave me, I have grown tired of this man's dictatorship! What does he think of himself? You have had enough already. He doesn't even allow you to mingle with other women, he has kept you tied to the pillar of our kitchen like a slave, I bet he gives more freedom to our maid than he gives you.' I tried to look into my Amma's eyes, they were dewy, so were also mine, but mine were red with anger, 'I can't take this anymore, Amma! I can't. I do not want to be a mathematician!'

At this there was a moment's silence. Then all of a sudden, Appa said, 'You will do exactly as I command you to do!' He marched ahead and as he completed his sentence, dug his walking stick on the floor, establishing a final seal on his decision.

I hated that style of his when he wanted to have the final word; I kicked the stick with my right foot, and my Appa who was leaning completely on the stick lost his balance. My arrogance-filled action made everyone hold their breath. Appa's eyes glowered. The veins on his forehead were almost on the verge of erupting. He lifted his stick to hit me, 'you son of a ….' I stopped the stick with my left hand, in my defense. With the other hand, he tried to slap me hard. I used my other hand to defend myself. Appa could not believe what had just happened. He was one of the most feared and respected men, his word was will for many and now his own 18-year-old son had humiliated him in front of everyone.

Defiance.

This was the biggest blow to his stature, to his ego.

I looked into his red eyes, there was disgust in them. I did not care to notice any pain or regret in them.

'This boy will never come back to *MY HOUSE… TO ME until I am alive, if he comes to my house; he will have to walk over my dead body.* Let him come the day I die, to do away with my funeral.' His eyes diluted, the eyeballs trembled as those words came out of his mouth, rather heart.

'*I will make sure that I come back to burn your dead body! Goodbye!*' I replied.

Everyone was shocked at the turn of events. I loosened my grip over my Appa's hand and stick. I left both and turned around. I walked out of the auditorium. Maybe a woman cried out my name or maybe a beautiful girl kept looking at me as I faded out into the distance, but I did not care. I had made my decision.

I marched ahead.

I had to catch the first bus to Madras- the City of my Dreams.

Goodbye Tuticorin!

Goodbye Appa!

23

1996
Madras

I was walking in and out of different production houses, sweeping the miles out of my days and placing stones on the comforts of nights, the same nights that I used to enjoy back home. Things had changed; life in the big city was, well, not a struggle. Life was much easier and fast, but not discomforting though, it was full of struggle. I was a hero back home, but here I was a nobody!

Almost 4 months in Madras, the capital of Tamil Nadu, I did not know if anyone missed me in Tuticorin. That fact hardly mattered anymore, for I had broken all bonds. Now I was a free bird, ready to fly high on a husky Sunday afternoon, the day when most people in the busy metropolitan city rested their asses at home.

I had no home in particular, for I was a runaway with just the thousand rupees that I had stolen from my father's safety locker. That money was reserved for food and emergency. I found shelter at the Madras Central railway station, platform no. 1. A Northeast bound train would wake me up at exactly 4:30 am. My bag that contained a pair of trousers and four shirts was my pillow. There was a *Siva* temple outside the station. I would take a dip in the temple tank. I had no time for rest, every morning I would get up with a bright hope on my face and knock on every producer's door and studio. Initially I began knocking at the doors of big ones like AVM, but soon I realized that it was impossible to find a chance among big names without a proper portfolio or a powerful background.

I met many other *aspiring actors*, during my quest to become one myself. They were people like me, trying to find a place among the elite, trying to make a mark for themselves. All of them were extremely talented; some were extremely handsome and divine in appearance. But we all had one thing in common: a pitiable fate.

I had made a friend or two with the sort of people who worked as connecting agents or *jacks*. One of them, a fat Kannadiga whom everybody called Gowda, was willing to help me on the condition that I would part with 60 percent of my first signing amount. Why would I not agree? At least, he was not asking me to sleep with him. I had agreed. Yes, there were people asking for such favors too. Startled me at first! Men enjoying men? What had the world come to?

After digging deep through his list of contacts at different studios in Madras, Bangalore and Kochi, he finally got an offer for me.

One of my favorite directors Mani Ratnam was producing a movie. Auditions were taking place at the Venkateswara Hall in downtown Madras. Tokens were handed to aspiring actors who had turned up that day for the audition, and my turn was 278. I waited for Gowda to arrive, for he had that magic wand by which he could simply erase the 7 or 8 from *278* and get me in sooner, much sooner.

Two hours later, when 27 of the persons had given their auditions, Gowda arrived, I noticed him from a distance, all credits to his reddish hair. He boasted that they were naturally red, but no one would take that for truth. Nevertheless, that was his signature, his landmark. The back of his head was bald and the skin was so damn shiny that one could see his face on the bald patch of his head.

Short, basely overweight with a plump face, Gowda was still lively. He did not walk, he waddled like a goose. I shouted out, 'Gowdaji! I'm here.'

He saw me waving at him and waddled towards me, on the way he got into conversation with someone. It was a tall stout man who was carrying a walkie-talkie in his hand. Then he smiled at him, shook his hand, bidding a gesture of grateful goodbye and started towards me.

'*Dei*! You want to stand here only?' He asked in Tamilian English that carried a *Kannadiga* punch.

'278' I remarked.

'You are next!' he mastered.

'No, its 27 now, next is ...'

'I am telling you, you are next, no more arguments.'

I smiled in responre. He must have settled it with that tall guy and got me in quickly through the backdoor. That magic wand of his literally erased a digit from my 278, I was now 28.

The next candidate.

After five minutes, I was standing in a tiny room sealed from all sides; there was not even a window that could let sunlight filter in. Just a door, through which I had entered.

There were six people in the room. Three were seated while the other three stood near them. Gowda went to one of them and murmured something into his ears and then went on to greet each of those who were seated. That was when I noted one of the seated persons. It was the man himself, Mani Ratnam, the man who had directed the best movie that I had ever seen, *Nayagan*, touted to be India's best film and is the only Indian film to be listed in *Time magazine's* list of Top 100 movies of all time.

I wanted to bow in obeisance, throw up my hands in praise and worship one of the demigods in the film industry. Would he make another *Thalapathy* with me? I doubted that.

The short supervisor summoned me. He picked the Reynold ballpen placed behind his ears and passed it over the paper that clung to the clipboard before marking a check in front of my name on that list. He turned to the person who was talking to Gowda, 'Let the next female candidate in, no. 29, Padmavathi Balachandran.'

He pressed a buzzer that was mounted on the teapoy near Mani Sir. I heard a bell ring outside the room but that was all. There was complete silence inside the room, as if there was no crowd waiting outside. I did not turn around to see who it was, as I was very excited and nervous at the same time. I was facing the panel of judges and had my back towards the girl. The sound of her anklets revealed the fact that she was drawing closer to me. My heart was beating faster than ever before.

Who was the girl?

What situation would be given us to enact?

How would I fare out in the task assigned to me?

Would I falter *en route*?

The man sitting next to Mani Sir discribed the situation and the scene that we had to enact. 'You are the son of a deceased public officer, now left on your own. You are in love with this girl, who is from an orthodox Christian family. Her parents would never let you people be together since you belong to a Hindu family. You are a year younger to the girl. Besides being jobless, your life is a mess, and you dream of becoming a filmmaker.' He said in a voice He paused to cough and then continued directing us, 'Your are *Karthik* and are trying to explain it to *Samantha*, why she should forget you and move on in life, even though deep inside you can't bear the pain of separation. Got it?' He asked, 'Both of you, ready?' he asked us as he exchanged glances with me and the girl behind me.

'Yes Sir!' I affirmed.

'Yes, Sir!' came a timidly sweet voice from behind me. The voice caught me by surprise and was rather a pleasant one. This one wasn't unknown. A voice had been haunting me for the past two and half years and it was this one. I knew I wasn't dreaming, but it could be a trick played by my senses for I was in great tension. I prayed to God it wasn't my imagination. I closed my eyes and turned around.

Slowly I opened my eyes, her figure revealed itself along with her shadow. The magical contours around her hips were familiar, I had seen them before. The pink silk *saree* draped around her waist went on to garner her beautiful bosom. I breathed in freshness; I needed it, as I finally let my eyes uncover the veil on her face. Chin like a swan drinking out of a spring, two shapely lips that cut through my heart and a nose that had the sharpness of a dagger. Then came the eyes, two black balls of sparkling moistness that rested in the nectar of the whitest of all oceans. Her skin was glowing like a golden incandescent bulb, which was more powerful than the helium blasting sun glowing outside harshly.

Her thick long braided hair fell to her knees. This *sreedeviness* had captured my imagination and had been holding me up against my will for such a long time.

I thought my heart had popped out of its socket in the chest. I walked in style towards her; the style was weaker than the mesmerizing lure that she generated. I noticed an expression of surprise on her face too, as my right hand slowly craned itself and ran silkily on her untouched face. The tips of each of my fingers caressed her skin, while she closed her eyes in seductive resignation.

The man was instructing something, but I could not restrain myself and listen to him.

'Samantha!' I exclaimed.

'Karthik, finally I get to see you again….' She replied.

I moved in, held her by the hip, my left hand embraced her curve. Butterflies fluttered all around me, in vivid shades of red, purple and blue. I did not remember Mani Ratnam anymore.

I dug my eyes into hers.

'I do not mind if you break my heart into two or a million pieces, I will bring another heart for you to play with! My body will keep on making hearts for you! If it fails to do so, I will kill myself and be born again to do so.'

'Shhhh….' She covered my mouth with her soft palm, 'do not speak like that.'

'I wouldn't let this moment pass even by a fraction of a second, let us live in this moment forever!' I pressed her navel with my thumb.

'If our parents do not let us live together, perhaps we should end our lives, this very moment.' She proposed.

'Dying is not a solution; I want to live with you. I have come a long way from home in search of my passion. Once I establish myself, I will come for you. Ask for your hand from your father.' I kneeled down, 'Wait for me until then, won't you?'

She nodded in affirmation.

'With whose permission has this love happened?'

'I do not know.' She said.

'Love needed no permission, Love is everywhere on this earth, if this earth and our love are true, we shall need nobody's permission to be together. But you must wait until I have made something of my life.' I pleaded.

She ran her eyes from my left eye to the right eye, 'Please take me away from here, I am not strong enough to resist my father and brothers.'

'Our love will provide you with the required strength. Just believe in love, believe in me.' I pressed harder and she almost broke loose. I held her tightly, then pressed her small head on my chest and kissed the top of her head. The smell of coconut oil from her hair filled me with eternal bliss. A tear dropped from my eye on her hair.

I heard something around me, was it the sound of rain falling on the roof? Where was I standing? I had forgotten. That is when I realized that I was standing inside a room and giving my audition for a role for a film that was going to be made. The sound was not of raindrops falling on the roof, but came from the hands of the men inside the room, who were clapping in appreciation of the performance that we had just given.

The man sitting next to Mani Sir rose from his seat and applauded warmly, I checked his face again; I had read or seen that face before in some film weekly. He smiled through his thick bushy beard, 'Wonderful performance! There was so much authenticity in your performance!'

'Thank you Sir!' I said humbly, still not able to believe what had just happened in the past one minute.

Performance? What? I thought I was living it.

'Though, the two of you got out of character totally and the dialogues seemed senseless, and my screenwriter here was continuously trying to interrupt and say the right words, you weren't bothered to listen. What man? Is she really the girl you are looking for?' he giggled with Gowda who was now standing with us.

'He is a great actor, Sir. Give him a chance and he will prove his worth.' Gowda pleaded with him.

'I am shortlisting you, young man. You have the potential to be the next big name in Tamil Cinema. We will call you if you are selected.' He smiled and then got back to the judging panel.

Gowda chuckled and looked at me, 'Ahaha! Awesome da! You have swept them off their feet. Come let us go now; I think you will surely get a role in this film.'

He did not say anything to the girl but she was ushered out too. I followed Gowda out of the room and knew she was right behind me. Gowda kept talking but my mind was keen on deciding what to say to Samantha, err… *Padmavathi*.

Finally, I knew her name. That was a huge promotion, from just a syllable to an entire name and the surname, which I was not able to recollect at that moment. Talking about promotion, I just hugged her, kissed her scented hair. *Did I cross any limit?*

I had my topic, I turned around and there she was timidly making her way out, stepping into a mosaic of aspiring actors. She was there, right in front of me. She looked at me and smiled gently.

'*Vanakkam* Padma.' I greeted.

'*Vanakkam* Thalaiva.' she blushed.

'I hope I did not cross any limit in that room.' I apologized while I rubbed the back of my head with my right hand.

She looked at the floor; slowly she put forth her left leg and with the toe started scathing the sandy floor. She ran her toe in shape of an arc, from one end to the other and back to where she began.

'Are you going to keep doing that?' I asked sarcastically, I was sure that she got my point. I wondered when she would stop doing that.

'You acted well.'

'Was I acting?' I retorted smartly, 'I was just being myself, said what my heart told me.'

She did not reply. She started walking past me.

I followed her quickly.

I crossed over and stood in her way, she did not stop walking, so I had to walk backwards. I wanted to ask so many things, could not as I was too excited to control myself. Yet I managed to stick to the minimum levels of decency, 'Hey..Hey...hey! Padma, isn't it simply fateful? I mean of all the times we have met, you disappear just like that.' I snapped my finger, 'And when I was totally unaware about the presence of a girl around me, you appear and I had to give my audition with you.'

'And you hugged and kissed that girl?' she demanded.

'No, I did not do it because that was just any girl.'

'Oh? So I am special, is that what you are trying to say?'

'Didn't I give you enough hints?' I laughed at my smartness. Well, I presumed myself to be smart.

She stared quietly for a moment, which gave me some tension and made me rethink about what I had just said, but all of a sudden, she joined me. She solemnly revealed her shining white set of teeth as she laughed like an angel. There was a *Raaga* in the way she laughed. *Sreeraaga.*

'*Kaapi?* I offered.

She nodded.

I was in love!

24

After saying goodbye to Gowda, I took Padma to my favorite hangout zone in Madras, The Indian Coffee House on Thyagaraj road. They made the best vegetable cutlet and coffee. We still called it *kaapi* over here and it cost just 5 rupees. World's best coffee for five rupees, it was a steal!

Two hot tumblers of *kaapi* placed on the table that lay before us. The blush had disappeared long ago. Padmavathi looked like a typical South Indian girl though her outlook was far more modern than I had ever imagined. It would have taken ages to convince a girl to accompany a stranger like me for coffee, but here she was, with *kaapi* and me. Well, of course, no girl would ever refuse a chance to go out with me, but this was not just any girl.

This was her.

My dream girl.

I managed to start a conversation, 'So, You came all the way to Madras for the audition?'

She took a sip of coffee from her mug, placed the mug back on the table and looked at me, 'I live here, dear.'

'Oh, I thought you lived in Madurai, remember the two times we met before?'

'Well, it's more like *three* times.' She said.

'Three?' I retorted, 'no way. We met twice, once in 1993 and then two years later in 1995. Both were weddings.'

There was a wicked smile on her face, 'You are right about those two, but we had met one more time as well.'

'No way, I am quite sure.' I declared but I was confused, 'Are you sure?'

She nodded, 'Remember *Subramaniam maama's* wedding?'

I tried to recollect.

She tried to send out hints, '1986, Madurai?'

'The one where the groom was from America, an NRI? Was it? And the wedding was postponed because they couldn't find a *varamaala*?' I asked.

'Well, that was my uncle, my *Amma's* second brother. In other words- My *Maama's* wedding.'

'Damn! I was only eight or nine years old back then, but I do not remember having met you then. I swear.'

'You remember some little girl trying to throw a *varamaala* around your neck. Insisting you should marry her?'

It all came back to me, 'How could I forget that? Oh God. Wait, was that you? I was so scared. I had to hide inside the lady's common room with my mother so that I wouldn't encounter you.'

She broke into a loud laughter.

'So much so, I almost….' I had to stop there.

'I almost, what?' She asked curiously.

'Never mind.' I tried to evade.

'Come on, tell me.' She insisted.

I could not tell her that I had *wet my pants* out of fear. I was a kid back then, a real innocent kid, and that girl who was sitting in front of me was a crazy little doll who kept running after me for 2 hours with a *varamaala*. I tried my best to change the subject, 'You remember, that *varamaala* was for the bride, and the wedding was almost brought to a full stop because you refused to return the garland.'

'I was a six year old girl. My mother told me that it I could marry the most beautiful boy I would meet there and that *dream* had brought me to that place. Little did I know that it was a joke. I'm sorry dear; I really did not want you to wet yourself.'

'*What?*' I recoiled, how did she know that? Did she read my mind or had anyone leaked out my little secret?

'I was just saying it, like an idiom, you know? Why are you so shocked?' Once again, she raised one eyebrow. That was an irresistible gesture.

'No, of course not. I did not expect a magical encounter with the girl from whom I had once hidden in fear. It's mesmerizing, the way you carry yourself, after all these years.'

'Tell me about fear. You pulled it off so bravely there.'

'Thanks.'

'At first I was nervous when I saw Mani Sir sitting among the *judges*. Totally nervous!'

I did not respond and in fact, I was sitting like a statue with my eyes popping out as if I had seen a ghost.

She shook me, 'what's wrong? Are you okay?'

I stood up suddenly, shaking the table, 'Oh! Shit.'

'What happened?'

I looked at her, 'Mani Sir!'

She looked back.

I continued explaining, 'I was so excited at encountering you in there that I forgot about Mani Sir. He was sitting there and I did not even go to him and seek his blessings before coming out of there. Damn!'

'So what? Sit down. it is ok. He liked your performance. Besides, do you think he really had time to talk to you? There were around 500 people out there.' She tried to rationalize.

'Do you think I should go back and….'

'Sit down.'

'Yes.' I nodded.

I sat on the chair.

'So what brings you here?' She asked.

'Huh? Oh, cinema. It is my dream to become the next big superstar.'

'And your academics?'

'What about it?'

'I mean, are not you going to study futher?'

'No, cinema is my life. I was born for it' I declared.

'And what do your parents say about it?'

'They know nothing, too old fashioned to let their child pursue his dreams.'

'Of course, they want your future to be secure.' she said.

What? Was she on their side too? I tried to keep my ego away from hurt. I asked her, 'What about you? Are your parents okay with you giving auditions?'

Her focus was back on the coffee.

I pressed, 'Shouldn't I have asked that?'

'I haven't told them. Though I am sure, I will go for higher studies even if I do not get a break from the industry. I was just trying here. Not as seriously as you are.' She gave a naughty grin.

'At least you believe that I am serious.'

'Of course, I got that almost 10 years ago, when you hid behind your mother's *saree.*'

'Hey, cut it out. Stop teasing me.' I protested.

She smiled. She revealed her ivory white teeth and I could almost see myself on its polished enamel. I wondered which toothpaste she used, but unfortunately, I could not keep it confined to myself, 'Hey, do you happen to use *Colgate?*

'What?'

'What? Did I ask something?' I realized the stupidity of my question and reacted as if I was not aware of what I had just asked.

'I should probably be leaving now. *Amma's* waiting for me at home.' She stood up and prepared to leave. I left a ten-rupee note inside the folder with the bill. Soon we were standing outside; the streets of Madras were busy as usual despite the fact that a domestic cricket match was being plyed at the Chepauk Stadium. Maybe their team had been losing out the game again. It is the inherent trait of our fellow countrymen, support when they are winning, and criticize loudly the moment they start showing signs of defeat. Well, I do not follow cricket at all, my only love is cinema and now the girl who stood in front of me. I would have watched cricket had there been any involvement of cinema in it. Maybe in the future, there would be a *decent marriage of cricket and cinema*. I could only wish for such a thing.

She was warping the floor with her toe again, I could not understand her. Five minutes ago this girl was casually sitting and chatting with me and, had coffee, but now she was playing a different tune. What was this? Was she doing some kind of rehearsal for the next audition? But I loved her, both as a shy person and an outgoing one.

'I thought you were comfortable with me.' I asked her, intrigued by her behavior.

'Of course I am.' she replied quickly.

'Then why do you keep doing this thing with your toe. Doesn't that mean you are feeling shy or something?'

'Oh! I just get reminded of that stupid thing I did back in '86.' she smiled mildly.

I laughed at her innocent reply., 'Maybe it's time that you moved on. You know, I believe that someday things will change. Just like the seasons. A lively spring follows the harsh winter. *Seasons change* Padma, *Seasons change.*'

'Yes, whatever! I will see you around, bye!' she gave her right hand for me to shake.

'What? Do I have to kiss that beautiful hand of yours?' I winked.

'*ahahaha,*' she hummed in her Tamilian tone, the same tone she had adopted a year ago when she had caught me eating mutton chops inside the cooking area of some wedding hall. She grilled me, 'Very smart, but remember you are still vulnerable.'

'Vulnerable? Who? Me? What do you mean?'

'Never mind, I've got to go, Goodbye!' She turned around and started walking.

'Goodbye!' I bid her farewell too. But I wondered why she found me vulnerable and to what. I looked at the sky and gave a moment's thought. I heard her speak again. She had turned around.

She said 'Pepsodent, I use Pepsodent.' She smiled.

Soon she disappeared from the fragrance, but her scent and aura lingered.

It never left me.

That is it. Finally, I was in love.

I wished for the rain to fall, so that I could dance in that rain, let my feelings out in the open and share my happiness with everyone. Sing out loudly and dance, just as they did in the movies.

And lo, soon the bright shining sun was enveloped by a thick cloud cover and in a few minutes, it started raining heavily, much to my surprise. Alas, I could not dance or sing as I had imagined. And later that day I saw the news that the cricket match had been called off without a single ball being bowled that day because of the sudden rain. Continuous rain had left the pitch muddy and the city cheerful.

And that was the beginning of a beautiful relationship which I wished would never end. I cherished every moment that I spent with her. She was the love of my life. However, she was not my first priority then. I desperately wanted to get into the film industry and was still trying.

25

1997
Madras

I waited for quite a long time to receive a call from the production house. Some people told me that they had already started shooting for that movie for which I had given audition. I refused to believe them. I had given a dozen more auditions after that. Though all of them said good things about my acting skills and asked me to wait until they called me up for a second round of audition for the short listed candidates, then nobody did. I was always shortlisted; but I would never receive any second call. Maybe Gowda was not trying too hard.

I was running out of money, soon I would start starving. I desperately wanted a breakthrough, but it was just not going my way. Gowda had found another young kid from *Hosur*, he was busy with the young boy. Apparently, he had realized that I was not attractive enough for the moviemakers. Maybe I was cursed; I must be bearing the curses of my *Appa*. I could not go back, but I did remember my mother's words. She had said years ago, 'Never rebel against your *Appa*, if he curses you, you will never be free of that. No matter how many dips you take in the *Ganga*.'

Maybe she was right. I was cursed. I wished to reverse certain things, but things that were already could not be undone, just like letters typed on a paper in permanent ink. If you type anything wrong, you have to tear the page off and start afresh. But how can I start my life afresh?

Months passed, often I met Padma at the Indian Coffee House, but every time we met, she would find me more frustrated than before. I was so broke, that she had started paying. There were no more smiling faces or toes that engraved the floor.

It was a humid day in August; the two of us were sitting at our usual table. After all these meetings, I had suddenly started finding Padma quite irritating, her way of talking about her dreams and then listening to my wishes and then trying to console me whenever I would break into frustration. At times, I would just feel like getting up and leaving, but then would change my mind, control my anger and stay with her. I would just sit there, without paying attention to what she would say, simply nod. Once again, she was trying to console me, 'Krishna, I can very well understand your frustration, but you have to stick to your dreams. Try harder.'

I nodded as if I had heard each word that she uttered and completely agreed with them.

'Krishna, why are you nodding, I know you are not listening to me at all.' She shouted.

'What do you want me to do, huh?' I shot back.

'Stop pretending, I just want you to stop pretending.'

'Pretending? You know, all these days, you have been lecturing me. Do not do this; do not think like that, try harder. Hell, I know all these things.'

'Krishna,' her tone had softened, I looked up at her, and her eyes had a tender expression in them. She continued, 'all these years, I had been waiting to meet you and when I did, I thought I had my dream come true.'

'What?'

'You think I am this liberal with all the boys I meet? No dear, I do not even talk to other boys. No sir, you are the only idiot whom I talk to. I have wandered around this city with you. You think I do that with every other guy I meet during auditions?' It was like a slap on my face.

'I'm sorry, I did not realize it. I am in a mess.' I confessed. I had tears in my red eyes.

'That you are. *A big mess*, but you still have time, loads and loads of time. You can always go back, start afresh. For once in your life be smart, think wisely. I am not asking you to forget your dream of becoming an actor, I am just asking you to place that on the backseat for the time being, and' she continued, 'study something. Complete your graduation in *anything*, get a decent job. Secure your future. Once you are working somewhere, you will have some money and then you can go for auditions. I am sure you will be as good looking and much stronger then. In fact, this depression on your face will disappear and you will be able to perform better.'

'I am not going back there.'

She sighed, looked around and then retorted, 'Try something here, work somewhere, save some money and then pursue...' she sighed again, 'We can always work it out, *together.*'

'What? Whoa...whoa...what do you think of me?' I bounced off the chair. What she said had clearly hurt my ego. I yelled at her, 'You think I am helpless? Huh? Do you think that I cannot make it in this city? You think I am so desperate that I am depending on a 17-year-old girl? If it is *YES* that you are expecting to hear from me, then I am sorry to disappoint you, Miss. Padmavathi Balachandran, but I am not depending on you. I will find my way out. I do not need you, your advice or that grumpy old man back at home who has been dictating my life ever since I started talking.'

I got up from my chair, put my right hand into the rear pocket of my trousers and brought out the red leather wallet. I pulled out two 10 rupee notes and threw them on the table and yelled, 'This one's on me and *this is it.*' I told Padma, 'We won't be meeting again unless I become somebody!' and I rushed out of the old building. I did not even bother to look back at that girl whom I had adored so much once, whom I had been longing to meet for 2 years. The girl whose face I would search for in every wedding that I'd go, the girl whose name was always a mystery and yet with that mystery I would weave dreams and net fantasies set in the land of fairytales.

Yet I had ended it all, asked her to stay out of my life. I had walked out on her; rather I had walked out on myself. Little did I realize then that I was being engulfed by the demon created out of my own ego. I had grown arrogant and what I had done to Padma showed the extent to which my arrogance could go.

As I charged off to my resting area, the Madras railway station, I saw a brand new movie poster fluttering around the edges of a press building. The poster had all the big names on it, Superstar Vijay, Raghuvaran. The same production house... Was it the same movie? Yes, it was. My heart skipped a beat, where was my name? He had said that I gave a wonderful performance.

Wonderful performance! There was so much authenticity in your performance!

There was another handsome young boy but that wasn't me, I had heard it from some of the other *aspirants* that he was the son of some Kollywood bigshot. That was the moment I realized that my dreams were about to get shattered, one of the first tremors had been the poster. My eyes filled up quickly, my teeth were set and with a trembling hand I picked up a huge stone that was lying on the corner of the footpath where I had been standing. I aimed at the face of the newcomer on the poster and shot the stone with all the power propelled by my frustration. The stone did not hit the poster at all. Instead, it got deflected in mid-air and hit the glass window of a nearby building. The glass shattered just like my dreams. Before some person from inside could spot the culprit, I decided to leave the scene. I was not getting anything right. I could not even throw a stone properly without breaking a window.

I am cursed.

26

That night I went back to the railway station after drinking some local rum. I was totally out of my mind. Somehow, I managed to stagger to the last bench on platform number 1. I was so drunk that I was not able to feel my body and surrendered to unconsciousness.

I dropped on the bench, hit my lips hard on the surface of the bench and that's all I could remember.

27

The next day
Madras

The next day, I woke up to find myself inside a police lock-up. Apparently, I had broken some laws but I did not remember which ones. I opened my eyes to dizziness. It was definitely a hangover. I had never tasted alcohol in my life before, so it was the first time. They say that the first time is always memorable. I wished I could remember mine and in fact, I could not. One of the constables walked toward the cell where they had locked me up, he stared at me and asked, 'Had a good night's sleep?'

I could not move, I thought somebody had cut off my limbs. There was acute pain in the region around my abdomen. I looked at my abdominal region and that is when I realized that they had stripped me. I was sitting there naked, not a pinstripe of loincloth over my feeble genitals. I was shocked, I somehow managed to move my hands and cover my genitals with them. My eyes filled with tears again, and I shouted, 'What the hell have you done to me? Ahhhh…' My lips hurt as I spoke; I felt saltiness in my saliva. I touched my lower lip with the index finger of my left hand while the right hand tightly covered my pubic region. I saw blood on my finger, my lip had broken, that is when I remembered the moment I had fallen unconscious. I had hit my lip on the bench.

The constable unlocked the door of the cell. He was carrying a pair of torn trousers and dusty shirt. He threw them inside the cell. He said, 'Dress up without uttering a word.' He commanded. The man was almost the age of my father, around 52. He had a thick moustache, a dark skin piled up on a very sparre body. quickly I picked up my clothes and wore them. They smelled like vomit. I wanted to throw up, but was scared to do so. I covered my nose. It took me more than ten minutes to wear my clothes; I could not move my right elbow or my hip without supporting myself against the wall. Maybe they had beaten me up last night while I was unconscious, just like that, for fun. The constable called me.

I stood up, shakily, started moving. Luckily the door was open; I did not have to apply any effort there. I felt so powerless. As I walked, I felt that the whole of my back hurt.

He pointed his *lathi* to a spot near his table, 'stand there!'

The constable raised my chin with his *lathi*. Slowly he moved my face to the right and then to the left. Both time, he examined my cheeks carefully. He spoke in a loud voice, 'So, what is your business here?'

I did not reply.

My silence had irritated him, but I was wise not to reply. He hit me with his *lathi*, this time the cane stick fell on my back that was already hurting. I screamed in pain.

'What the hell do you think these places are? Huh? You think that it is your bedroom. The country's free and the road's public so you think you can sleep on the footpath?' He asked. There was fury in his eyes.

'I...I...' I tried to defend myself with words but he was not ready to listen.

'Shut up, you know this city is filled with *bloody bastards* like you.'

'I am not a *bloody bastard!*' I shouted. For a moment the

physical pain did not hurt me at all, the emotional pain had given me strength to shout against the furious constable.

'If you had a legitimate father, you wouldn't be lying drunk in railway stations at midnight.' The constable surfaced.

'I am not a *bloody bastard*!' I repeated with a little less anger than the previous time.

The constable noticed the tears filling up my eyes, he suddenly realized that I was about to surrender. He sighed, noticing the helpless anger that I had displayed.

'How old are you?' He asked calmly.

'Nineteen.' I replied.

'What were you doing there?'

'I was trying to get a night's sleep!' I cried desperately.

'On the bench? Where do you live?'

'I do not have a home. I left it a year back.'

'What? Who is your father, what does he do?'

'My father is a crazy old man; he is a maths teacher in a boys' school.'

'Where?'

'Tuticorin'

'Tuticorin! And what are you doing here then?'

'I ran away, I wanted to become an actor. I came here.'

The old constable put his hands on his waist and uttered a sigh. He asked my name, 'What is your name?'

'My name is Krishnaprasad…' paused '…Iyer'

'Wait until I report this to the Police station in your town. You are not going anywhere but home, young man.' He ordered once again, 'Don't you have any shame? You have brought so much disgrace to your family by running away at such a young age. An age when you ought to be cramming for exams, you are here drunk and lying unwittingly on railway station!'

'I do not care, I am nineteen, and I am an adult. I have the right to stay where I want. If you do not let me go then…'

'Then… What?' He interrupted.

I looked around, there was a door a dozen feet away and since it was early, there was no one standing at the door. All I had to do was gather enough power to propel myself out of that door and away from the police constable. I took a very deep breath, the constable said something, but I did not hear it. I stood like a statue for a moment. The constable was observing me silently. But before he could say or do anything, I ran out of the room.

He stood there speechless. He jumped up, but by that time, I had pushed aside a few uniformed men and was running i knew not where. I kept on running. I knew my joints would give up soon, but I decided to use this energy as long as possible so that I could get far away from that police station. And in that haste, I couldn't hear any whistles or yelling policemen charging after me. I simply kept running.

I took a few turns and before I knew it, I was standing in front of a plain horizon. A great sea loomed in front of my weary eyes. I dropped myself on the sandy shore. I had run miles, maybe for hours with that single burst of energy. I fell on my knees. It had started hurting again, but before it could stagger me with pain, I lost consciousness.

I was hearing something; in fact, I was hearing many things. I was seeing faces.

I kept hearing and seeing them one by one.

They were flashbacks. I was hallucinating.

'Krishna, I can very well understand your frustration, but you have to stick to your dreams. Try harder. That you are. A big mess, but you still have time, loads and loads of time. You can always go back, start afresh. For once in your life be smart, think wisely.' Padma said with bifocal spectacles resting on her nose, a ruler in her right hand. She was reading them out from a book. I was being lectured. She continued tutoring, *'Complete your graduation, get a decent job.*

Secure your future. Once you are working somewhere, you will have some money and then you can go for auditions.'

'1986, Madurai? You remember some little girl trying to throw a varamaala around your neck. Insisting you to marry her?' A little girl revealed her face from a veil. She looked cute and she was holding a garland of flowers in her hand.

'I am shortlisting you, young man. You have the potential to be the next big name in Tamil cinema. We will call you if you are selected.' A short man said. There were other people around me. Some of them had very serious faces, while others had no faces at all. The words kept on echoing inside my ears with each rising decibel.

'Thalaiva, Look at this. Super-figures, Thalaiva!' exclaimed a joyous Kanna, whom I had not heard from in a year. I realized that he had grown a beard. Has he grown older than I have?

'How dare you use force on your father?' my father grunged against something. He lifted a *lathi* and hit me on my naked buttocks.

'This boy will never come back to MY HOUSE… TO ME until I am alive, if he comes to my house, he will have to walk over my dead body. Let him come the day I die, to perform my last rites.' The old man grunted. Everything around me started burning.

'I will make sure that I come back to your dead body! Goodbye!' There was an explosion. That is all I heard, all I saw.

Soon everything started fading out. Maybe I was dying.

Maybe I had fallen asleep.

I had found myself a new place to sleep.

28

1997-98
Madras

That incident got me on all fours. I decided that I must find
some kind of work for myself, a job to keep myself from
starving. I had to keep myself alive. I had a dream to rebuild, a
dream that had been shattered into tiny pieces. I kept away from
the Railway Station and its surroundings. I would be careful every
time I came across a police officer. I did not want to be caught. I
did not want that old constable to catch me and dispatch me back
home. I often wondered if he had informed my parents about my
whereabouts. I hoped he had not.

I went for several interviews but nobody was interested in
hiring an undergraduate. Even worse, nobody was willing to
hire an 11th pass runaway. However, all those interviews were
for office jobs. Therefore, I decided to loosen my stiffness and
try for *lesser jobs*, jobs that demanded more of physical labor
and less of mental strain and *a heavy sacrifice of one's ego*. The
kind of jobs where uneducated people would be preferred over
graduates. Where graduates would not even think of sending in
an application.

Frustration grew inside me and being jobless had started
attracting some really bad people. But I kept myself away from
them. I had started smoking heavily now.

The beach where I brought myself to sleep was the hub for smugglers and drug addicts at night. I fought hard to keep myself clean. I had three options open before me. The first was the blue Bay of Bengal. She would always call out my name, asking me to merge myself in her untamed depths thus, putting an end to all miseries.

The second one was to join one of those people who were selling drugs, become an addict myself and take temporary relief from *physical suffering* by losing myself into the world of intoxication.

And the final one was to go back home, which I would never do. Not because of my ego. The circumstances had killed and buried my ego deep within those sandy shores of Madras. It was the fear of losing my father. Every time I wished to go back, those words would repeat themselves inside my mind's jukebox.

I will make sure that I come back to your dead body! Goodbye!

I missed my family, my mother, Kanna, all those people and last *but the most*, my Appa. I wanted to call Kanna and ask how things were going, but lacked the courage to do so.

I was lying aimlessly on the beach one night. Foamy waves from the ocean swept my feet, keeping me alive. There were very few souls on the beach that night. Nevertheless, I loved the isolation. Loneliness gave me company. I looked at the bright moon hovering in the dark sky. It was so beautiful, more so because it was alone in the sky. There was not a single star to give company to the patchy white sphere that night. I felt myself merging in the heart of the moon. Some writer had written in his masterpiece that everything had a soul. The earth and the moon also had souls. I wondered if my soul could talk to the moon's soul and find some kind of a company there.

A few minutes later, a couple arrived at the spot where I was resting. It was a middle-aged man and a woman, presumably his wife. They sat there at a distance of 6 feet from me. I guess they had not seen me. They were talking.

The man put his right hand around his wife's shoulder and pulled her closer to him. He spoke in a guttural voice, 'I think I will miss him a lot. I wish I could have saved him.' The tone was one that of brief sorrow.

'You were unaware, his time had come. He had to go. You tried your level best to save him.' She consoled him; her voice was thicker, quite unlikely for a woman of her kind.

'Yes, after working for ten years with him. I feel as if I wouldn't be able to start another day without him.' He sighed.

'People die. You got to move on.' She replied in the manner of a *wise woman*.

He rested his head over hers and looked ahead, 'I do not know whom they *will hire now*. I hope it's somebody as good as he is.'

My eyes popped open. All my senses quivered outside my body. I had just heard something which made me rise up suddenly. The couple was taken by surprise. The woman shouted in fear. The man barked, 'Who's that?'

I wiped off the sand from my hair.

'Somebody is hiring?' I asked him.

'What?'

'Right now, you were saying something about hiring someone. I would like to take that job, whatever that is.' I offered.

The man was confused, 'you wouldn't want to…'

I interrupted 'I do not care; I will take that job, Please!' I begged.

'Okay, fine! Meet me outside the Madras City Municipal Corporation's Sewage plant at 8 am. I will talk to the supervisor.'

'Thank you Sir.' I took the hands of that man, shook it vigorously, and saluted his wife, 'Thank you madam, thank you.' I said. My eyes filled up once again with tears. Unlike previous ones, these were tears of joy. I finally had a job, 'tomorrow morning 8 am. Municipal Corporation. I will be there Sir, I will be there.'

I started jogging away from there.

The man asked from behind me, 'By the way boy, what is your name?'

I heard him meekly, though I yelled back gleefully, '*My name is Iyer, Krishnaprasad Iyer.*'

29

December 19, 1997
Madras Municipal Corporation Building

The night passed in a joyous state of sleep. I had never slept so peacefully in recent times. The hope of getting a job the next morning filled me with a kind of rigorous calmness. My life was broken, now I would be getting a chance to fix it. I was awake at five in the morning, the beach felt fresher than ever. The cool breeze from the Bay of Bengal kissed my yawning face. The scent refreshed each living cell inside my withered body.

I had been standing outside the Municipal Corporation building since seven in the morning. The man from the beach had asked me to arrive outside the building at eight. I was there an hour earlier. I wanted to impress him with this act of punctuality.

At around quarter to eight, a thick-skinned blackish male wearing a *khaki* uniform arrived outside the gate of the building. That khaki was clearly not a police officer's uniform. I made sure by rechecking. Maybe he was a peon at one of the divisions in the huge building. I had seen the same man at the beach last night. There was no woman with him. He was coming towards me. I smiled at him. He did not bother to smile back. As he came closer to me, he pulled out a folded page and handed it over to me. I quickly received and unfolded it.

It was a form.

'Fill up the form quickly and give it back to me.' He commanded as he produced a packet of local *beedis* from his shirt's pocket.

'Okay, sir!'

'And yes, attach a passport size photograph with the form. Do you have one?' He looked at me while lighting the *beedi* with a matchstick.

I bristled through my wallet, there had to be a photograph there somewhere. I kept a couple of my photographs all the time in my wallet. There it was, a rusty black and white photograph of mine, taken when I was in class 10th. The inseparable smile on my face cast a shadow of irony over my bewildering face of the present. I wondered if the very same photographs were displayed on notice boards in police stations of Tuticorin too, among the list of *MISSING PERSONS*. I handed the photograph over to the man in khaki.

'Fill it up fast. We have to report downstairs by 8 am.' He blurted among blusters of raw tobacco fumes. He coughed lightly.

'Well, yes, of course!'

It was an application form for a government job. I filled it Proudly.

'Very good!'

He started going through the form that I had just filled up. I added meticulously, 'I can also speak English and Hindi.'

He gestured by raising his hand as if asking me to shut up, 'You do not need to know any of these to do what we do here.'

I was confused. The man blew out another ounce of smoke from the handmade *beedi*. He started walking towards the rear side of the building. He gestured me to follow him. I kept pace with his short strides; I did not overtake him. I was right behind him.

There was a wooden door a few feet away from us, but startlingly the man with me was not going that way. He did not stop at the door; instead, he stopped a few feet ahead. He had stopped in front of a hole in the concrete floor. He called me over. I had stopped walking after reaching the door, so I started moving towards the man in khaki upon his gesture. A look of amusement eclipsed my face that he ignored. He kneeled down and then with a small careful stride he stepped inside the hole. I moved closer and kneeled down. It was an entrance to the world below. A foul smell hit my face. I placed my hands around the perimeter of the hole and slowly pushed my right foot into the hole. There were steel steps embossed into the walls of the ground below. The staircase to hell, I assumed and started my journey *downstairs.* The smell kept growing in foulness, and so did the pressure of the stinking air inside the hole. They would always say that hell was a rotting place to be. This must be it then. The sound of flowing water ascended as I descended. What was this place?

The smell of beedi was successful to some extent in keeping the stink from blowing up my nose, but now it was not helping either. I looked at the man who was descending just under me; he had thrown the *beedi* away. I wished that he would light up another one.

A few minutes later, we were all standing at the *zone.* The man pulled off a yellow safety helmet from the hanger on the wall. He wore it on his grizzly haired head. He threw another one towards me; I caught it and wore it. He walked towards me, put a hand on my shoulders and spoke, 'It's unlikely that people take up such jobs. People like white-collar jobs and they get paid more. We do the real thing of cleaning up the city for such a low pay. It is a dirty job, only desperate people end up here. I talked to the supervisor; he agreed to keep you for fifty rupees a day. Ten hours duty.'

'But what exactly do I do here? I still did not understand! I thought it to be some office job, like on the *ground floor* and all.' I demanded elusively. The smell of some kind of weird gas blocked the smelling path of my nose.

'We refine sewage waste down here.'

'Refine?'

'We clean *shits* of the entire city. Janitors.'

'But...but...I signed up for some government job, you only gave me that application minutes ago, remember?'

'What do you think this is? Some kind of a multinational private venture? Hell, we are government servants working for the Municipal Corporation of Madras.' He spat out the words into the smelly air.

'You did not tell me that I was going to clean shit!'

'I was trying to, but you did not let me finish. You were too desperate. You were willing to do any work, remember?'

'Yea... But this. Oh my God! Can't you get me any other job? Don't you have friends *upstairs*?' I suppressed.

'Yes, they either ask for certificates and entrance tests or demand lump sum in bribe for blinking an eye. If you have either, you may try *upstairs*. I know a few guys who can help.'

'Huh! What kind of a choice is that? I do not even know if I have passed 12th or not. How can I sit for their tests?'

'This one's dirty, but at least you will have something to do. It's difficult to live in the big city, why don't you pack your bags and go back to where you came from.'

'I am from this city.' I lied to the man.

'Of course and I come from America.' He grinned sarcastically, 'Look here, boy, people arrive in packs in this city everyday to try their freaking lucks. Few of the lucky ones find their dreams, few find some other way out, few go back unsuccessfully while the left ones go berserk in desperation. The choice is yours. I saw desperation in your eyes last night.'

'Was not it too dark for you to see?'

'Was that a joke? Anyway, I talked to the supervisor and got you in because I thought that you needed this work. At least you had not decided to take up wrong kind of jobs, *yet*. However, it is your choice, you may decide against it. I won't force you; I will tear off your application and throw it away into this flowing sewage water.' He pointed to the stream of dark viscous liquid flowing behind him.

That was where the smell and the sound were coming from. It would have formed a beautiful sight if there had been no litter residue in that incoming stream of water. I thought for a moment. I needed silence to think. The noise under the earth was surprisingly soothing to the ears, there was the kind of silence I needed. I began pondering over things.

I had no money, no work and could not go back. Sometimes words said had lightning effects and I did not want such words to come true. I did not want to see my father dead. I could work there in that dirty rotting hell until the time I was selected in a film. I could save some money too, enough money to bribe one of the *friends upstairs.* Alternately, I could get out of here, go back to Marina beach and lie there until some miracle took place and I became the king of the world! Maybe this was another test that I had to pass.

My father's curse.

I had made up my mind.

I had decided.

Once again, I had made my decision; I wished that it would not falter like the previous ones. I fixed the helmet on my head and requested, 'Can I start now?'

The man smiled and pushed his right hand forth, 'Welcome to the team, I am Thangaraju Wincent.'

I shook his hand, *'My name is Iyer, Krishnaprasad Iyer.'*

30

1998 - 2010
Madras

Life took a turn that I had not expected. The boy who ran away from home to become an actor in the big city became a janitor. Fate forced me to *refine sewage water*. I worked every day, did not skip it. In the beginning, it seemed difficult and tacky. The smell and sight of live fecal matter and rats running below my feet gave me nauseating fits. Nevertheless, it became part of my life. However, a few months later, I got used to it. It grew in me and I worked without feeling hurt. During my early days, I would give auditions on Sundays but as usual, they never followed up. I grew tired of giving pointless auditions; maybe I was not actor material at all. I started skipping auditions and went around the city on Sundays. I would work on Saturdays too; it gave me an extra day's pay. I was not sleeping on beaches and railway stations any more. I had a bed of my own in a tidy room filled with bachelors. They accommodated me at the staff quarters. Though small, the room was satisfying enough for my needs. I had made new friends, they liked me and I liked them too. As time passed, I forgot my dream somewhere. I almost bumped into Padmavathi a couple of times in the city. I did not want her to see me, ask me how I had been doing. I had an answer, which would put her on the seat of victory. She had asked me to go back, I did not and now I was a nothing, she had definitely won that covetous *bet*. Whatever happened, life had to move on and it did.

I had worked there for two years as a janitor when one of my roommates came up with a public scheme. The State Government of Tamil Nadu was encouraging undergraduate public servants to take up *correspondence graduate courses*. Courses were offered in B.A and B.Sc. Completion of such a course would make the candidate eligible for higher posts in the State Government offices under some kind of reservation that I could not understand then. I signed up for *B.A English* and worked hard for the next three years. I dribbled physical labor in the daytime and mental labor at night. I blocked all sources of entertainment. I had to graduate and find a job *upstairs*.

God had given me a second chance.

Finally, I graduated in 2002. I was the only one to graduate in the first lot out of 35 others who had tried with me.

It was celebration time.

In 2003, I got a job *upstairs*. I passed a clerical test and was appointed a clerk in the mayor's office. There was a change in routine life. I got freedom from the stinking nether worlds of Madras. Oh Sorry, I mean *Chennai*. Madras had changed into Chennai now, just the way a rebellious egoistic teenager from Tuticorin had changed into a satisfied young government employee.

I had changed. I missed my family, Kanna, my mother and above all my father. But I was afraid to go back. I was completely satisfied, but deep inside, one thing strangled my satisfaction. I had not told anyone around me about it. They knew about my past but I never gave them any hint about my fear. I buried it deep inside my mind, maybe it would fade away one day, just like my dream of becoming an actor had faded away. I had no news from their side, neither was I in touch with any of them. I had completely forgotten about Padma. She was no more even a part of my vague memories.

I had moved on.

31

May 20, 2011
Municipal Corporation Building, Chennai
12:00 noon

I had piles of pending files on my desk and half of them were dusty and decades old. This was one of the moments when I wished that I had never become a computer operator at a public office. I should have never gone for that computer course in 2007. Because of that additional *qualification,* I got promoted to the post of computer operator and was responsible for feeding all manual data entries into the computer database. What was worse was the deafening fact that some of those entries were made prior to the independence of our great nation, centuries before that fateful day of 15 August 1947. My fingers showed some kind of reaction after touching some of those really old files.

I was working on a file from 1987 when Thulasidas, one of the peons, came to me. He was from *Palghat*, Kerala and hailed from a Tamil Brahmin family just like me. Though he was quite fluent in Tamil, he often carried a colloquial *Malayali* accent especially when he uttered bilabial syllables, typical of those who spoke Malayalam.

I had not called him, so I raised my pencil and asked him to leave. He did not leave. I stopped typing on the computer and looked at him. I raised my eyebrow in an interrogatory style.

He answered in his colloquialness, '*Yaaro ungale meet panre vandu irrukku Saar.*'

'*Yaaru?* I replied in *Tamil.*

'*Oru* couple *Saar. Oru paiyyan, oru* madam. *Ungale teriyumnu sollerei.*'

'*enge?* Where?' I asked trying to figure out who that would be.

'*Inge ninthu caféku poyaachu. Ange wait pannere avar.*'

'*Avargalude per yenna?* I asked.

The young peon scratched his head, '*Saary, Saar.* I forgot to ask, *Saar.*' He apologized in typical Palakkadan accent.

'Okay, you may go. I will check.'

The peon walked away from my desk. I yawned and slowly got up from my seat. I started walking towards the exit.

Yaaro ungale meet panre vandu irrukku Saar. The peon had said that a couple had come to meet me, but who could they be? I had friends only from the city; they would generally call me up on my *cell phone.* Who would come to visit me at my office? I was not in touch with any of my relatives or people from my past.

Could it be Padma? Had she found out about me? A Couple? She must be married by now, had she come here with her *husband*? Why would she want to see me if she was married? Maybe she was only engaged and she was here with her fiancée. They must have come to invite me to their wedding.

My guts tingled. The dumb peon had forgotten to ask the person's name. *Saary Saar,* he had replied when I asked him the person's name and identity. None of us Tamilians got it right, the whole of India said sorry and sir while we still pronounce *saary* and *Saar.* Hope the coming generation would improve its accent. Who were they? Why was a couple waiting for me at the cafeteria? Slowly my heart started beating faster, the blood was trumpeting through my viens.

My heart kept beating as fast as it could. Heavier every passing second, when it was on the verge of exploding, something vibrated above my ribcage, just where my heart was pumping. I thought that was it! My heart had given up, exploded! But why was it singing *enna thavam seithane?* It was the ringtone of my cell phone. I stopped walking, sighed and exhaled. Then inhaled a deep breath of air. I pulled out the ringing phone from the pocket of my shirt.

Martin calling.

It was my insurance agent, Martin. I was getting my motorbike insured.

'*Macha*, Where are you?' the voice blasted on the phone.

'At the office…' I responded coldly.

'I am waiting for you at the café, when are you coming down?'

'What? You… at the caf…Wait a minute!' I juggled my thoughts back to where it all began, 'You sent the peon? He said some couple was here to see me, waiting at the café.'

'Yes, I reached here, had been trying to ring you up, but it would not connect. Therefore, I caught one of your peons. I had to get you down here somehow, did not want to disturb the *decorum* of your office by coming in. I told him that I was your insurance agent.'

'Did you? He said he forgot to ask! Damn it, that idiot. I am coming there in a minute. Man you got me killed with tension. Too bad you weren't covering my life insurance.'

'Hahaha…Ok, come down quick!'

'Ok *macha*, coming. Bye!' I hung up the phone and started striding at double pace.

32

The Café, Chennai
12:12 noon

Martin was standing at the entrance of *The Café*. We shook hands. I was not expecting Martin that day at all. I blurted out what I thought, 'What are you doing here? We had to meet next week, right? Is... is everything all right?'

Martin followed me inside. He walked towards the last table in the corner on the right side, four chairs around the table. Somebody was already seated there.

It was a woman. She had her back towards me. Martin had already taken a seat; he sat facing the two people. Suddenly that vague enigma crept back inside me as I paced quickly towards the table. I wanted to see who that woman was. I reached the table, crossed the seated woman and turned around. Now, I saw her. My heart once again pumped blood at four times the normal rate into my veins.

A tanned face, splendidly sliced pair of lips running pink to crimson naturally, hair cut short to form bobbing curves around the neck. And the eyes, thick black in an ocean of white surrounded by thick and long eye lashes. I knew those eyes; I could never escape the earthy gaze of those beautiful eyes. My heart froze for the next few seconds, this was her. However, initially I had thought it would be her but after receiving Martin's phone call, I had ruled out all the possibility of it being *her*.

For a moment, she had made a comeback into the world of my thoughts and here she was, sitting in front of me, wearing a golden brown *saree* and red sleeveless blouse, the woman who was the girl whom I once loved.

'Padma!' I said unwittingly as if I were speaking in a trance under the effect of a hypnotic spell. Indeed, I was hypnotized. Enchanted by the sudden appearance of this gorgeous woman. The woman whom I had desired for a long time in my life. She had not lost it at all, in fact, she had only grown more beautiful; add to it a reckoning sense of style.

Martin woke me up from the trance, 'Hey, why don't you take a seat?'

I nodded, pulled out the chair and sat down on the chair next to Martin. I was facing Padma. I noticed that she had a tint of seriousness on her face for she was not smiling at all. I tried hard to start a smile but to my astonishment, I found my lips and the muscles around my mouth paralyzed. I could not move it. What was I feeling? Happy? Confused? Shocked?

Yes, I was confused. What was she doing here? What was Martin doing with her?

Finally, I gathered all the nerve I could and sustained a sensible query, 'So? How long has it been?'

'Fourteen years!' came a blunt answer from the woman sitting in front of me. Her voice had thickened. She was not that 17-year-old girl anymore. She was 31. The *sreedeviness* still lingering around her lips clashing between the brows.

'How... how are you?' I stammered.

'What an incredible journey life has been! Hasn't it?' her tone had changed; no more did it sound blunt. A sudden sharpness had crept in. There was anger in the voice that followed, 'A young boy, everyone expects him to be something, but he runs away from home. A rebellious young boy chasing his dreams!' She scolded. I kept examining her for signs of marriage, any kind of rings or *mangalsootra*. I did not find either. Was she still unmarried? Meanwhile she continued chiding me, 'Then all of a sudden he decides to cut off from everything and everyone. There is no news of the boy. No news of the boy for fourteen long years! What does he think he is? Lord Sri *Raama*?'

'What?' I choked.

'What are you looking at? You are no *Raama*, got it? But there is someone who deserves to be summoned as *Bharata* today.'

What was she talking about? She made no sense at all. Why was she pulling in characters from The *Raamayana*? I was not on an exile for fourteen years because I was never going to go back home. This was my home now. Was she about to call herself *Sita*?

'Look, I …' I stuttered but I was interrupted.

'*Anna!*' A voice caressed me from behind. All the hair on my body stood up, juices poured in from the adrenal medulla. My eyes opened wide in astonishment. That tone and that sweetness could come only from one person. I stood up and turned around slowly.

33

Kanna.

There he stood. He was not the little boy that I had left behind in Tuticorin, 15 years ago. This Kanna was a man, broad shouldered, tall and stoutly built.

I baby stepped towards him, he was taller than I was. I was six feet tall; he stood an inch or two higher. My eyes filled with tears. Whether they were happy or sad, I had no idea, as there was a sudden rush of emotions. With trembling hands, I touched his cheeks. Thick blades of uncut stubble kissed the inner side of my palm. His dark skin shook with an unbearable sensation of finding a lost one.

'*Kanna!*' I finally uttered a melodramatic whisper.

He nodded and then burst into tears. How much more could I restrain myself from giving up? I gave up and hugged him tightly.

'Anna, why did you do this? You could have at least thought about me, of all the good times we had.'

'What are you saying? I think about you all the time, every moment, every second and with every breath. I just did not have the courage, *Kanna.*'

'I wanted to come earlier, much earlier, but I did not want to hurt your feelings in any way by breaking my promise.'

'How did you find me?' I enquired as I released the young man in his mid or late twenties.

He looked at Padma and explained, 'You remember *Padma akka,* don't you? We met her years ago. At a wedding.'

'Yes, yes!' I nodded, but little did he know how much more we had known each other, at a *level persona.*

'Well, *Amma* had asked me to contact *akka's* parents if they could look for you in Chennai. We were all hoping that you would be in Chennai only. Since *akka's* family had settled in Chennai for a long time, we thought that they could help us. Though our hope was infinitesimally minute, but still we hoped. Rest was her mission.' He smiled at Padma with sparkling eyes.

Martin had shifted to the seat next to Padma so that I could sit with my cousin, *Kanna.*

We sat down.

Padma continued explaining from there onwards, 'The first thing that I did after getting Hari's request was something anyone would do, give a Missing Person advertisement in local newspapers. We used your old photo there. I was quite sure that sticking up an outdated photo would hardly help people in identifying you. Especially, since you have changed so much *physically.*' She looked at my face and then turned towards Martin, who was sitting next to me, 'Luckily, one of the readers of *Chennai Sethikal* recognized the name and details of this particular person who had run away from Tuticorin around fourteen years ago. *Someone* who had access to all the personal details of the great *Krishnaprasad Iyer,* and that *someone* is sitting right here in front of me, Mr. Martin Gonzales. He called me.'

I looked at Martin; he was smiling shyly as if he had been acknowledged for tracing the most wanted criminal of the world. He tried to justify his action, 'Hey! I was in two minds after I read that piece of news. And I was really shocked; you never told me that you ran away from home!'

I did not reply. I know he was trying to put back the blame on me. Of course, I was worth the accusation.

He continued speaking, 'I tallied the few details that had been given in the advertisement with the insurance papers that you had filled in last week. They matched- The address, father's name, mother's name, date of birth etc. At first, I was a little reluctant to give out your location but then I had a weird intuition. What if these people had some terribly strong reason for seeking you?' He crossed his hands and fixed his gaze on me sharply, gargled his throat and said, 'and unfortunately I was right.'

'What do you mean?' I asked.

Martin did not reply. He fell silent and so did everyone. Padma tried to look the other way when I turned towards her.

Finally, I turned to the one whom I could always count on, *Kanna*. His face was dipped in a syrup of heaviness. I could now clearly read the seriousness behind their intention to seek me after such a long gap of fourteen years. He looked down at the top of the table and then raised his dark mature face towards me, those dark eyes charged with salty tears. With a very heavy monotone, he revealed the reason, '*Anna!* Your *Appa,* is not well. After you left, he had taken to drinking like anything. He got expelled from school for teaching under the influence of alcohol. He spent all his property and money on alcohol.'

I was shocked to hear this; I knew my father was one of those people who would never even touch alcohol. This was all because of me. I had not just left Tuticorin; I had left my father hapless.

I wiped the sigh on my face and asked, 'Why didn't you get to me earlier?'

'We wanted to, but he had clearly stated that if any of us tried to bring you back, he would hang himself. He still held on to his words seriously. Remember those last words you had said to each other at that wedding?'

MY HOUSE... TO ME until I am alive, if he comes to my house, he will have to walk over my dead body. Those words echoed around me. Just like his son, ardent on his words.

'Shit!' I cried.

'We thought that you might come back someday, but neither your ego nor his wanted to lose this battle!'

It was not my ego. I was scared to come back. I said in my mind. I could not say that outside because no one would ever believe me. My heart had started beating at double the rate once again. It pounded hard against the walls of my chest. The thumping sound could almost rock the tables around me. I felt the pulse in my ears too.

Kanna continued, 'Six months ago Appa had a stroke, the doctors were able to get him back to life. They had asked him to stop drinking. However, he was not done with punishing himself. Two weeks later he was drinking again, worse he had started smoking too. Anna, your house lost its peace forever. Last week he was found lying unconscious in his room, he would not wake up at all. We were scared to death. We took him to KMS in Tuticorin. They detected some weird condition of his health because of heavy drinking.' The tears started flooring down from his eyes.

'I left my father to die!' My heart started giving up too. I was praying that Kanna did not push away all chances of hope now by saying that *he was indeed dead.*

'He isn't dead. KMS people asked us to move him to Medanta in Gurgaon, near New Delhi. Only they could take this case up. It is a rare kind of surgery which is performed in only two or three hospitals in the Indian subcontinent itself.'

I sighed, closed my eyes and breathed in and out.

'When are we taking him to Delhi?' I asked him.

'He has been admitted there already. But they wouldn't carry on the surgery unless we pay them. The insurance cover was used up in his last stroke.'

'How much is it?' I started calculating all my savings and bonds that were about to mature. I believed I could come up with a good figure. I had saved for an apartment in Chennai.

With a heavy heart, he said 'Eight lakhs!'

'*What?*' I blew out of the water. I had not assumed anything that would exceed two lakhs. This was four times more than what I had assumed. I had made such an assumption after carefully calculating every paise that I had with me.

'Your *Appa* had no money with him; your *Amma* sold all the ornaments that were left with her. Most of us contributed but are still falling short by 6 lakhs. Many of our uncles simply backed out because of the fact that he had been very rude to them lately. They said that he had no right to live anymore because even if he was saved this time, he would keep drinking and again he would be admitted. It was better to let him pass away. But *Amma* insisted upon saving him. She believed that you might be able to help her out and so, we are here.' He thrust his hands on the table.

'Damn it!' I shouted as I rose up throwing my chair backwards on the floor. Tears filled up my eyes and they were falling drop by drop on the granite floor. 'What the hell have I done?'

'He never blamed you or anyone for his drinking habits.' Kanna tried to drive away my guilt.

'You know who is responsible for all this! We all know. Just… just… just tell me what do I do now?'

'The money…'

'Yes! Yes, I will get the money.' I declared.

'Are you sure?' Kanna checked.

'I am!' I knew I would have to beg from a few more people than I had anticipated, but I know I could arrange that amount. I would break all the bonds, even the ones that were not mature yet. The banks would charge me with high rates of penalty for breaking immature bonds. But I had to do it. I had to make it up for my father. I am the reason that has left him half dead and now I must bring him back to life.

Martin patted on my back, 'Hey brother, I will arrange for some hassle free sum as soon as possible. Just do not worry.'

'We are all with you, Krishna!' said a calmingly sweet voice. It had been Padma. I stared at her with red eyes. I wanted to apologize to her for my arrogant behavior shown fourteen years ago. I wish I could take back those words that I had said which ended our short-lived relationship. I smiled, my tearful eyes acknowledging her efforts. *Words*, all those words I had said to Padma took her away from me. All those words that I had said to *Appa* were now taking him away from everybody.

Just words! Words of hurt! Words that hurt. Why did I have to say all those words?

Martin pressed my palms warmly to notify me of their presence.

Padma got up from her chair and took leave, she reasoned, 'Krishna, I will have to leave you now. I have to pick up *Lakshmi* from school. '

'*Lakshmi?*' I asked.

'My daughter.'

'You… you are married?' I asked in shock.

'Well, *seasons change*, don't they? Goodbye everyone, I will see you later.' She turned around and started leaving.

Seasons change. But she was not wearing anything that showed her as a married woman. No ring or *mangalasootra*. There was no mark of *kumkumam* on her forehead, the symbol of every Hindu woman's marriage. I looked at Kanna, startled.

'She got divorced two years ago.' Kanna explained noticing the surprise on my face.

That was the second most depressing news I had received that hour. As I looked at her leaving through the door of The Café, a melancholic strain passed through my soul. Deep down that melancholy, I felt responsible for her divorce. Maybe she could not let go off me. After all, First love is *first love*.

I got back to my current priority which was gathering the requisite amount of money and getting to my father who was admitted somewhere in Delhi. I asked Martin, 'Hey, can I depend on you for the tickets too. I need to pack up my stuff and fetch some money.'

He agreed, 'Hmm... Would you like to leave tomorrow?'

'Make it tonight itself. I do not want to waste any more time here.' I turned towards Kanna, 'book two tickets in any class.'

'*Anna!* I cannot make it. Not right now. My wife is expecting our first baby anytime this week. I could only come after...'

'*What?*' I could not believe it! My little Kanna is not little anymore, 'Hariprasad! I am so happy for you!' I cried. This was the first time ever I had called him by his real name, Hariprasad. He had always been my little Kanna, but now he had grown up. I could not decide which way I should let my tears flow. There were both tears of pain and joy. I hugged Kanna tightly once again.

Padma was right, *Seasons change.*

34

Chennai Central Railway Station
06:25 pm

I returned to my quarters with Kanna. He helped me with the packing. We talked for a little while about all those years we were together and the years we were not. Kanna left for Tuticorin in the evening after tea.

Martin had booked my ticket and had arranged around one lakh in cheque for me. He promised some more money by next Tuesday. I was more than grateful for whatever help he had already given to me. I felt burdened by this gratitude. He drove me to the railway station in his Maruti Swift. My train was to arrive at about fifteen minutes past seven. Martin could not stay for a long time at the station; he had to attend a client in Ambattur.

After he had left me at the station, thoughts came bouncing back into my mind.

Thoughts of fear, guilt and pain.

That sudden fear rose once again which had held me back from going home all these years.

This boy will never come back to MY HOUSE... TO ME until I am alive, if he comes to my house, he will have to walk over my dead body. Let him come the day I die, to do away with my funeral. Appa had said.

I will make sure that I come back to your dead body! Goodbye!

Why did I have to say that? I could have apologized instead of striking back in that language, the language of our unbending egos.

Should I go? Would *Appa* die the moment I step into the room where he is? No! It's impossible, I am just being paranoid. This is superstition. I must not give away my mind to such unscientific and baseless fears. My leaving him has brought such a fate unto him. Only if I get back can I bring him back to normal. Why did I have to leave?

'Damn it! Shit!' I cried out loudly, and this sudden burst of emotion attracted everybody's attention. All those people who were present around me gazed at me as if they had seen a madman. Indeed I was behaving like a mad man. I sat on my briefcase. I pressed my right palm over my forehead to pinch my stress. My heart pounded faster, again!

I started walking from there. I wanted to stay away from people till at least I got in to the train. I wanted isolation. Strangers made me more tense. I reached one end of the platform. There lay a stone bench, lonely and misty in every sense of the world. This was the same bench where I had slept for months, all that time when I was struggling to find a break.

Nostalgia.

I moved towards the bench, I gently bent to touch the surface of the bench. It had grown coarser and dirtier than I had known. A small drop of saline water dropped on the dirty surface of the bench. Meanwhile, an announcement was made in the station, the train was to arrive in a few moments and before I could know it, it had arrived. It was time to leave. But everything was coming back to me.

The big old Grand Trunk arrived at the Chennai Central railway station majestically. I checked the list that was pasted outside the compartment. My seat was confirmed. Thanks to Martin and his friend. I stepped into the train with my briefcase.

Briskly browsed through the seat numbers and finally found my seat. Seat no. 63, I had the side seat. Three teenagers and four bachelors were travelling with me in my *coupe*. There was a beautiful woman in the next coupe and almost everybody was interested in getting her to notice them. She would give a tough competition to all those men when they try to sleep. But I was least interested, my mind was preoccupied.

Fifteen minutes later, the train had started moving. I bid goodbye to the big city. The train had set on its next journey. A journey that will take me back to my dying father.

A journey that would end it all.

A journey, that would see me argue and fight it out against my own fears.

A Journey of Hope.

35

May 21, 2011
Somewhere in Southern India
03:15 am

Everyone in the coupe was fast asleep, some men were dreaming lustily about the bodily amusing middle-aged lady from the next coupe while others were simply asleep. All the lights were down inside the compartment, the only source of illumination were the passing track lights outside. I rose from my throne and slowly walked towards the washbasin located at the rear end of the compartment. I pressed the lid of the tap upwards. A stream of water poured down on my hands and rest of them hit the metallic sink. With my right hand, I gathered few ounces of water and splashed it on my dried up face. I repeated this process four times until I could feel my drowsiness fade away into the night's darkness. I released the lid and the flow of the water stopped. I moved towards the door, pulled down the latch with my right hand. My muscles almost tilted the axis of the latch. The door unlocked and I pulled it backwards as I rested my bottom on the door that had opened behind me.

I looked outside, it was dark, the moon was hard to find among the school of dark clouds, but there was some whiteness at a spot. I recognized it as the lunar marvel trying to peep in through the clouds that had gulped it.

As I dwelled upon the happenings of the past, both long unforgotten ones and the forgettable recent ones, I produced a cigarette from my pocket and placed the filtered end in my mouth. I screwed the lighter and there was a spark, which went off in seconds, another try, and this time the lighter produced a bright flame that did not extinguish. I brought my face closer to the flame, there was the earthy smell of tobacco catching the first flames and soon the cigarette was ready for *consumption*. I turned off the lighter and placed it back in my pocket.

'What if *his* words came alive?' I thought as I puffed in a few vapors of tobacco.

'Oh God! Please find a way out, I do not want him to die! O Lord of Tirumalai, help me!' I prayed.

I exhaled a weave of smoke into the atmosphere. I looked at the *K* engraved on the wrist of my right hand.

A tear fell from my eye.

As the Sampark Kranti Express passed over Krishna Bridge, my heart passed through a bridge that separated hope from fear. Dawn was still awaiting its final call before the night could shed out every inch of its eerie darkness.

There was some hope in the darkness, the hope of a bright dawn waiting on the other side.

Moreover, all I needed was some more hope.

Part 3

Revelations

36

May 22, 2011
Ghittorni Metro Station
08:45 AM

The fat man stared at the empty paper cup that he was holding in his hands. He had finished the cappuccino an hour ago, but he did not throw the cup away, instead he kept holding onto it. Jai was yet to finish his. He had hardly made it half way through. He got so involved in Iyer's story that he forgot all about the cup of cappuccino in his hands. Iyer had a pitiful expression on his bulky face and shook his head in despair. He turned his head to Jai and began speaking, 'All these years, I just compelled myself to believe that my father didn't care for me. However, the last two days have revealed enough things to counteract all those years of abrasive thinking. I deduced that I was a fool! A big fat fool!'

'Wow! I... I still can't believe it!' Jai succumbed.

'Believe what?' Iyer asked.

'A number of incidents from the story you narrated. However, the most impossible one was the tug of war against your *Appa* at that Muslim wedding. It is difficult for me to digest that incident.'

'Why is it so difficult to digest?'

'Come on! You do not look like somebody who would hit your own father! Your face looks quite innocent for that matter.' Jai said.

'*What is written on a face?*' Iyer sighed thoughtfully, 'Look at me! What was I and what have I become now?' He handed Jai a photo from his wallet. It was the same black and white passport sized photograph.

Jai took the photogroph from him. He observed the boy in the photo. He was young, handsome and in his late teens. 'Is this you?' He asked while marveling at the boy's handsome face.

'That *was* me!' The fat man corrected Jai.

Jai handed the photo back, 'you were handsome then...' he said as he tried to match the face in the photo with the one in front of him, 'You have changed a lot. It is natural, I guess!'

Iyer sighed. 'Can I ask you something?' he asked hesitatingly.

'Shoot!'

'Would you do me a favor?'

'Hmm...' Jai thought for a second and then agreed, 'Okay! But what is it?'

Iyer pushed his right hand into the pocket of his shirt and pulled out a neatly folded white envelope. A blush passed over the dark skin of the fat man. He held it close to his chest and started explaining, 'This envelope contains all the money I could arrange. A cheque for five lakhs,' He moved the envelope towards Jai, 'Would you give this to my Amma. She's at Medanta Medicity.'

Jai was puzzled at this strange request 'But why can't you...'

'I am scared!' Iyer interrupted, 'What if those words came alive?'

'What? What *words?*' Jai recoiled in his seat.

'Those parting words, *I will make sure that I come back to your dead body!* That is what I had said! My last words to Appa. All these years those words have haunted me... kept me from going back home.'

'Are you crazy?' He pounded heavily on the back of the seat.

'I just do not want him to die, especially since he is in a critical stage!'

'It is *Two thousand and Eleven A.D*; you cannot be so much superstitious! I mean, damn it! Give me a break!' He exasperated at Iyer's explanation.

'I'm scared!'

'You think that your father will die the moment you step in front of him? Just because of those stupid things the two of you said *fifteen* years ago?'

Iyer nodded shamefully in agreement.

'He is gonna die anyway! You know that? The only way you can save him is by getting that cheque in there! Do you get me?' He held Iyer by the shoulders and shook him, 'Do you get that?'

'Please! Please! Do not force me! You just hand Amma this cheque for my sake. I cannot go in there! It might sound like mere superstition to you, but I just don't want to take any chances. Already I have troubled him a lot.'

'You are impossible!'

'Just take this and hand it to Amma, please!' Iyer requested the teenager.

Jai sighed and accepted the envelope containing the cheque from Iyer, 'All right! I will do this for you!'

'Thanks *da*!' he said gratefully.

'But you will come with me to the hospital, right?'

'Okay! But I won't step into the building.'

'Sure!'

'Do you know where it is? Medanta Medicity?'

'Oh Yea! It is a famous place in this region, one of the best in the country.'

'How far is it?'

'It is in Gurgaon, will take about an hour from here.'

Krishnaprasad Iyer got up from his seat and proceeded towards the door. Jai collected his bag and remembered that he had run away from home and probably his parents were looking for him all over the city with the cops. If he went back to the city, He would get caught.

'Hey Listen!' Jai called Iyer.

Iyer stopped and turned around, 'What is it, boy?'

Jai did not know how to put up his point to that man who had just narrated his life story without even caring to know the boy's real name: if it were really *John Abraham*. The fat chap definitely needed Jai's help and his problem was very genuine. Jai's problem could be tackled if he sneaked out carefully. How hard would it be to dodge Gurgaon Police? Jai decided to go with the man and help him out. Grant his wish!

Iyer was still waiting for Jai to speak. Finally, Jai dodged, 'Please let me buy the tickets for us!' He smiled.

Iyer smiled back and opened the door and went out. Jai followed, while going out of the room he felt a strange emptiness. He turned around. The Pathan was still there. Jai had got himself so engulfed in Iyer's narration that he hardly noticed anyone else entering or leaving through that door. The bulky man smiled and led Jai.

37

Jai and Iyer walked towards the ticket counter and Jai quickly purchased two tickets for Huda City Center. The woman at the counter produced a fake smile as she threw two tokens through the small opening at the glass interface. She stared at Jai for a moment as if she was trying to recollect something that had crossed her mind. Jai felt weird. He started walking away. He turned around and she was still observing him carefully.

'Weirdos!' Jai whispered into Iyer's ear as they walked away from the counter.

A few feet behind, the woman inside the ticket counter shook her head.

'Weirdo!' She said to herself while observing Jai.

The two started walking towards the security check. The station was still as empty as it had been two hours ago. There was hardly any movement inside. Jai was the first one to go under the scanner. He came out clean, and then he was asked by the police officer to place his bag on the conveyor belt that would pass the bag through an X-ray machine. Security measures had been tightened up in all parts of the country especially in those places where the Indian Premier League matches were being played. Delhi was one of those places, playing host to the Daredevils. Delhi Daredevils played Pune Warriors a day ago and today Chennai Superkings were scheduled to meet the Royal Challengers from Bengaluru. Jai was a diehard supporter of the Delhi based franchise. He wondered which team Iyer supported or whether he watched cricket at all. A majority of middle aged and orthodox people disliked the whole idea of clubbing the game of cricket this way. They thought it to be *divisive*.

What the hell? This was entertainment, sport and *edge of the seat* excitement packed into a single deck.

Jai's bag came out of the scanner. He picked it up and put it on his back. Iyer was already waiting for him. Jai wondered if the security people had checked him at all.

'Did they check you?' he asked.

'They were busy on their radio!'

'Yea right!'

They stepped on the escalator that went upstairs to the platform. The train was already awaiting departure. They made it in time. As soon as they stepped inside the train, the doors closed automatically. There was an announcement and soon the train was in motion. The two took a seat near the door itself. The entire train was almost empty.

'Maybe they will fill up in the next station. Gurgaon is still 20 minutes away!' Jai said.

'You would know better.' Iyer said.

A brief silence followed during which Jai kept on looking at his new acquaintance off and on. Something about him did not make sense. Was it that his story that was similar to Jai's own life in many ways or was Jai missing something?

Finally, Jai broke the silence; he asked Krishnaprasad Iyer, 'Tell me do you watch the IPL?'

'What?' Iyer seemed to have come out from some kind of a trance, 'What did you say?'

'IPL, do you follow IPL?' Jai repeated his query. Clearly, he was trying to start a conversation with the bulky man about something that did not remind him of his lamentable past.

'*Namma Ooru Chennai,* I support Chennai Superkings *da!*' He claimed joyfully like a little kid who had just been asked to select his favorite flavor of ice cream.

'Oh! They are playing tonight!'

'Is it?'

'Yea! They face Bengaluru tonight.'

'I never liked cricket, it was always cinema for me. I started watching cricket because of this IPL thing. It brought cinema and cricket together. But I am not that excited about it this time.'

'Yea! I do not need to be an astrologer to read that. I am sorry I was just trying to keep you away from unwanted thoughts. You get what I mean?'

'I am glad that you tried. Not many people have done that for me. I remember actor Vijay sporting yellow in the first edition, but now nowhere. But now I think Suriya is the best actor in Tamil cinema. I used to be jealous of him in the past, especially when I saw his face on that poster of his first movie. It could have been mine.' Iyer said with a hint of gloom in his eyes.

'Look! Whatever happened has happened. There's nothing you can do about it. Never do anything like that again. I don't know, I cannot explain. Okay? Just understand what I just tried to tell you.'

'Life has to go on. I realized it quite late in my life. I hope I can set an example for someone else.'

I guess you already did, thought Jai.

'Ok, tell me just one thing, what was it between you and Padma? Were you like *dating* each other?'

'Dating?' The man was hearing that term for the first time in his life for sure.

'Going out together, you know, like boyfriend and girlfriend. Get it? Dating?' Jai explained as he crossed his index fingers.

'She was a very good friend. I loved her… I think so. However, I gauged my love for cinema at a much higher altitude. I did not realize how important Padma had been to me at all. Even after we decided never to meet again…'

'You broke up!' Jai corrected.

'Sorry?'

'That's what it's called. Break up is the word. When you break a relationship. That's when you *break up*.'

'Okay, and after we *broke up* I was not bothered to get back to her, apologize and at least continue that healthy form of friendship which we shared. It was my ego.'

'Wow! I just asked a simple question man, you have gone deep! Chuck it! I do not really believe in this love shit anyway!' He said as he picked his ear with his finger. The face of Tania appeared in his mind. How he had ended it with her and all those moments they had shared. He sighed, 'Love sucks!'

'You will say that now. You are young. You probably have other priorities. But fifteen years down the line, you'll realize that you had got all your priorities wrong.'

'So, you repent the fact that you missed out on love during your golden days of life?'

'Young man, the golden days of life began after I broke up with Padma.'

'What?'

'Yes!'

'But didn't you struggle a lot after you ran away from home?'

'Yes, but that struggle brought the good side in me. I might not have become an actor as I dreamt, but I became a successful individual. If I hadn't run away I would have to struggle with my academics, score marks, earn a degree and then find a good job for myself.'

'Like a sucking old maths professor?'

Iyer chuckled, 'But I ran away, I struggled on the streets of Chennai, I was bent and broken by the harshness of life. Instead of throwing up life, I started from the lowest point set by life and from there I began climbing up. I was a graduate with a Government job. I rode my way without any big hand on my head. That, my boy, is a tough task for any person.'

'Hmmm… I agree! I give that to you, you were determined.'

The computerized system of the metro coach made another announcement. They had almost reached their stop. The voice of a woman first announced in English, shortly followed by aother announcement in Hindi this time in a man's voise. Jai got up from the seat, 'Hey, we gotta get off here. This one is the last stop.'

'Is it?'

'Trust me!'

38

Outside Ghittorni Metro Station
09:00

Hussain was told by the telephone operator that the Lottery Office was open only till eleven. He had two more hours till eleven and waiting for the metro to restart its operation did not seem a feasible option. He finally decided to take the longer route, catch a bus. It would take at least 3 hours for him to reach his destination by road owing to the heavy traffic on the highway, but at least he would be there. He had seen enough maniacs like the teenager who had been blabbering continuously. The boy's face was engulfed by arrogance and ego. Hussain didn't like him. He was a simple man who lived by the virtues of the *Quran Saahib*. Arrogance and ego were both traits of the Qafir. He wasn't one, he feared Allah, more importantly he believed in Allah and his faith stood steadfast in all phases of his miserable life. Every Friday he would donate wholeheartedly at the Masjid to feed the poor. He himself would stay hungry for the night, but would never skip charity. He believed that anyone who earns must understand the pain and serve the one who's needy. He was a man of values and imparted the same into his son, Arshad. He would never want his son to be like that teenager.

He rushed out and walked towards the bus stop that was almost a mile from the station. He knew which bus he had to board.

39

Bhaktawar Singh Chowk, Sector 38, Gurgaon
10:11 am

They got off the train, took an elevator and were outside the station after few minutes. Jai crossed the busy road. Traffic was always very heavy outside the Huda City Centre Metro Station. This was the point of convergence for almost half a million Gurgaonites who had to commute via the Gurgaon Metro Service. This was the starting point. Iyer followed Jai closely. The rush was less today because of the accident. Jai walked towards the auto rickshaw stand. An auto rickshaw was parked, ready to start, while four others waited in queue. Jai pointed at the auto rickshaw and instructed Iyer, 'We gotta get into this. We will get off at Bakhtawar Chowk and walk towards Medicity or catch another auto if it's tiring for you to walk a few steps.'

'It is perfect; I walk miles every day!'

'Oh Really?' Jai stared at Iyer's bulging tummy.

As soon as the two were seated, the auto took off. The journey took 10 minutes. They got off at the junction and took a right and went on the Bakhtawar Singh Marg. The traffic here was not much as this was one of the less populated areas of mainland Gurgaon. Besides, it was 10 am in the morning. Most of the people would be either at work or at school.

A temple complex stood upright on the left side of the road. One of them was painted black all over. This was a temple of *Shanideva* as the main deity. All temples in India where the presiding deity is *Shanideva* has this characteristic feature. The sun shone in through thick dark clouds on the black granite surface of the temple. Iyer prayed silently as they went past the temples. Jai observed his companion.

'Seriously you have a lot of faith in God?' Jai.

'Who doesn't?' he reverted.

'Hey! Talk for yourself!' Jai sounded indegnant, 'Just because you believe in your superstitions it doesn't make them solid science!'

'God is real; He is the ultimate science of everything! Today everyone is researching in different fields of science, but in the end all of them will find the same inference- God is ultimate science!'

'Why are we talking about this?' Jai cut the conversation short. Iyer was clearly disheartened at the boy's attitude. 'Look, if we walk a little faster, we can reach there in 5 minutes.' Jai informed.

'Sure!'

They walked faster and a group of closely new-age buildings with huge glass windows loomed before them.

'See those?' Jai asked Iyer.

Iyer focused on the buildings and nodded.

'That is Medanta- the medicity.' Jai told Iyer.

'Oh My God!' Iyer exclaimed in surprise, 'Is this really India?'

'I bet it is!'

'*Adada! Superu!*' Iyer exclaimed. He had never seen such a building in his life.

'Yea, whatever!'

'The metro, the malls, and those glass buildings, everything looks so much American! This place does not look anything like India.'

'But most of the people here are the same, narrow minded.' Jai remarked sarcastically.

'This place is beautiful!'

'You will find lot of South Indians in Medanta. All those nurses are from your part of the world.'

'Kerala! They must be from Kerala. Malayalees make good nurses. You will find Malayalee nurses all over the world.'

'What's the difference?'

'A lot! Language, food habits, culture.'

'Oh wait! Do you mean they don't speak Tamil? I thought everyone in The south spoke Tamil.'

'No dear, we speak Tamil, Malayalees of Kerala speak Malayalam, Telugu is spoken in Andhra and Tulu and Kannada are spoken in Karnataka. It is a huge country and we all have our little differences which make us one of a kind.' Iyer declared proudly.

'True!' Jai nodded, 'This whole area to the right was once used to be stronghold of the Jat community of Haryana but now Malayalees have outnumbered them. All nurses working at Medanta live here and it is almost like a mini-South…err…mini-Kerala here. There are two or three hotels too, one of my friends used to dine there frequently until he got a bug in his stomach.'

'He must have eaten beef fry, Malayalee hotels are famous for their Parotta and beef fry. I am telling you, both these things are not good for your health. The maida flour in Parotta and worms in beef are killers.'

'I don't know what he ate there, but it sure had to put an end to his dining streak.'

'My roommate is also a Malayalee, he used to have Parotta and beef fry regularly for dinners. He could not live without it. He was a Catholic, but never went to church.'

'See? There are people who do not believe in God.'

Well, actually, he loved a Muslim girl and that got him ousted from the local community. He was stranded. He would pray and confess in our room itself.'

'Oh! Hardly matters. When it comes to women and money, people tend to look over *God*!' he commented.

'Well, I looked over the woman for the sake of my dreams.'

'You are an item! A specimen from the museum of freaks! What else can I say about you?'

'Hahahaha!' Iyer heartily chuckled hearing Jai's words, 'Why do you say that?'

'Oh come on! You were foolish to have run away from home! I think that was the biggest blunder that you had committed in your life. You could have stuck a little longer at home, bear your *Appa's* attitude, survive everything and after graduation pursue your dream. You could have, you know?'

'What would *you* have done if you were in my place?' Iyer asked Jai.

'If I were in your place, I would have never…' Before he could complete his sentence, Jai realized what he was going to do that day! *He was indeed in Iyer's place.* He was himself running away from home, away from his dictating father, away from a life dominated by mathematics. He was running towards his dream of becoming a Bollywood actor. His story until now was not very different from Iyer's.

There had been just two points of difference, the place and the fact that Jai still had time to recover from his action. He still had time to go back. He gazed at the huge building in front of him; the clouds had parted and made way for the sun to shine brightly on the glass windows. The glare from the glass woke Jai up from his reverie.

'If you were in my place?' Iyer tried to know.

Jai ignored the question. He ran his right hand over his head and declared, 'Here we are. This is where your father has been admitted.'

'Okay, I will come *vunly* till here.' Iyer declared.

'Are you sure?' Jai confirmed.

'Positive! You please go and give that money to my mother. My father's name is Raamasamy Iyer. He is in room number 336 attended by Dr. Jaydev Singh.'

'Okay, let me give this then. I will be back soon. Don't worry!' Jai consoled and started walking away from Iyer.

'Young man, listen!' Iyer called Jai from behind.

Jai turned back and asked, 'Yes, What is it?'

'I don't know you or your name, but I would like to give you one small piece of advice. Take it from this stranger'

'Hmmm...'

'Never hurt your parents, their feelings. Especially that of your *Appa*. He has worked his whole life for you, sacrificing all comforts, and it's not wrong if he wants something minute in return.'

Jai looked down; a feeling of shame slashed at him. He had a lot to learn from this fat man.

Iyer continued, 'You know, this earth and our fate have something in common. They are both round! Where you start is... where you end. What goes around,' Iyer took a deep breath and continued, '*comes around*!'

Slowly Jai raised his head and looked at the wrinkled, fat chubby face of Krishnaprasad Iyer; an essence of deplorable wisdom reflected from his face. He had seen it all and had shown a part of it to Jai. Jai nodded in agreement. He had surrendered to Iyer's story. His eyes dilated. A thin layer of tears vaguely replaced the dryness in Jai's eyes. He smiled and praised Iyer, 'You are a good man, Wait here, I'll be right back.'

Jai turned around and started walking towards the gate. He walked towards the central building as told by the security guard. Soon, he disappeared into the building and the clouds reappeared in the sky. They covered the sun and the brightness was soon gone. It was going to rain again.

40

Jai walked towards *one of the many* receptionists. She was busy typing huskily on her keyboard. There was a sign hanging above her desk that read 'General Enquiries'. Other desks had different names on their respective signboards like General Medicine, Ortho etc. It was a busy place as he could see from the way people were running here and there around him- doctors, nurses, patients, and people! scurrying Impatiently through that corridor.

Jai went to the receptionist's tall wooden desk. She looked up at the teenager standing in front of her. Jai greeted her with a mild smile. She smiled back cheerfully, unlike the way the woman at the metro station had. The smile was genuine and never looked forceful at all, these women were trained look overtly attractive and to smile that way.

'Good morning Sir, How may I help you?' She asked in a chirpy voice.

'I....Well...I am looking for Mr. Raamasamy Iyer. He...He has been admitted here for....Ummm...' He jittered nervously. He did not know the exact illness. Iyer had not told him. Jai made up for that, 'Room no. 336, attended by Dr. Jay...Jaydev Singh, yea!'

'Are you related to the patient?' She said as she typed in some keywords on her keyboard.

'Oh...Well! No, I am not. I know his son. He is a...' Jai stammered for a microsecond and finally pronounced, 'He is a *friend* of mine. He sent me here to deliver something.'

'Oh! Very well, May I know your name please?'

'Yea sure, my name is Jai Sharma. Jai *Prakash* Sharma.' He said Prakash proudly, it was his father's name.

'Thank you dear, the patient's on 3rd floor. Take the elevator, then sixth room from the right.'

'Thank you very much!' he smiled gratefully.

'You are welcome!' She smiled back. Her breasts tucked perfectly in her white shirt, revealing just about nothing less than perfect fantasy.

He hated taking the elevator. He was scared of elevators and other enclosed spaces. One of his friends had told that he was claustrophobic. Indeed, he was, and as he stepped inside the elevator, the fear crept in. He pressed the button that read '3' on the metallic wall. The door beeped and closed, and the elevator jumped into motion with a shake. It scared Jai. He closed his eyes and breathed in deeply. He prayed for the journey to end quickly. Then there was a beep again. The lift had stopped. He exhaled in satisfaction and waited for the door to open. The door did not open for a few seconds. His heart started beating faster again. The air around grew thinner or he was feeling that way.

'Fuck!' he cried aloud.

He ran his eyes over the buttons. A button was blinking red. He pressed it instinctively, the blinking stopped. And slowly the door opened. He jumped out of the elevator. He sighed heavily, looked up, and gestured with his eyes. '*Oh God!* Hell! I will never take an elevator again!' He told himself. For the first time in years, he had mentioned *God* in his phrase. He had aligned with the atheistic way long ago and had never looked back since then. However, he did not note that. It came out accidentally. Instinctively.

He went past the first five rooms. He walked past rushing nurses and patients on wheeled stretchers. The smell of antiseptic went deep into his nostrils, nullifying his senses. He hated that kind of smell. He started feeling vaguely dizzy now.

A woman was standing outside room no. 336. She was not a nurse, she was an old woman dressed in a checkered cotton saree and had tender wrinkles on her tense face.

THIS MUST BE IYER'S MOTHER! Jai thought.

He was reluctant to ask her if she was indeed Iyer's mother. However, he did not want to peep into the room where Iyer's dying father was resting either. Going near a dying person would always freak out Jai. He was a weakling as his father had predicted earlier. Asking an old woman's identity was much simpler than knocking and entering the room of a dying man. Therefore, he called her, 'Excuse me mam!'

'Aa?' The woman responded gravely.

'Are you... hmmm...' He pondered over what to ask, 'Is Mr. Raamasamy Iyer in this room?'

The woman adjusted her thick spectacles and looked carefully at the boy, 'Who are you, son?'

'Uhh...I am...Well, Krishnaprasad Iyer sent me.'

An expression of shock and surprise clouded on her face, the wrinkles seemed to dance together in commotion.

'*Krishna?*' her eyes filled up quickly with tears, 'Krishna is my son, where is he?'

'He... he sent me with this.' He held out the envelope containing money to the sobbing old woman, 'The money you needed. He wants you to pay it off right away.' Jai was not able to stand there anymore. His knee began to tremble. He had never faced a crying old woman in his life before. In fact, he had never faced a crying person before, just his girlfriend Tania who had sobbed two nights ago when he had dumped her. He didn't have to face her either.

He did not know what to do, if he had to put an arm around her bent shoulders and console her. He never done anything like that; he did not know how to do that!

'Krishna… I want to see Krishna! Where is he? Is he all right?' She continued to sob.

'Look, mam! He is all right, okay?' Jai held the woman by the shoulder and looked straight into her eyes, piercing it with a laser of solace, 'He wants you to pay off all the required money and he will be here as soon as Mr. Iyer is safe. He will be here, *trust me!*'

She nodded continved.

'Now, please go and do what is required. Everything will be all right!'

'Yes, yes. Thank you, son. God bless you! Oh, would you please take this inside and keep it on his table?' She said and forced a basket into Jai's hand.

'Oh!' Jai did not want to sneak into the patient's room. His hands had received the basket involuntarily and the woman was already walking away towards the elevator with the envelope.

'Shit!' He swore.

41

Despairingly he waved his head as he turned the knob on the door and opened it. He entered the room. It was a spacious white room with the occasional presence of green. On the right hand side of the room, there stood a bed adjacent to the window. There was a table next to the bed. As he walked towards it, he noticed the face of an old man among disarrayed folds of a woollen blanket. Jai closed his eyes so that he did not have to see the dying man. On the way to the table, he hit the side of the bed and it made a thudding sound and shook the bed hard.

'Shit, holy shit!' He cursed himself.

He wondered if he had disconnected any wires that connected to the old man's body. He was of afraid if he had killed the old man accidentally. He held his breath and opened his left eye and carefully placed the basket on the table and prepared to leave. Slowly he opened his eyes and started breathing again as he turned his back to the patient. He was heading towards the door.

'*Kkk*...' He could hear something behind him.

Jai was shocked! His eyes opened wide.

'Kkrrris...Krisshhnn....hmphh....' The voice was bulled with a terrible anxiety and a binding feeling of attachment. It tried hard to say something, '*Krishnaaaa.*' It cried finally.

Jai's jaw dropped. He had seen today what he could not have imagined. He was being forced by his fate to face his fears. First running away, then elevator getting jammed, surviving the smell of the hospital, walking into a dying man's room and now being summoned by a dying man as his son in a comatore state.

He gulped and turned around.

'Krishna, you have come? I knew you would.' The grim voice creaked.

Jai did not know what to say, he moved closer to the man. He saw his face for the first time. It was not the face of a cruel dictator like Iyer had said. There was no thick moustache guarding a diabolic face. He was clean shaved, the white hair on his head were few and the face had the pallor of anemia. Thick dark circles rimmed the closed eyes. The man was speaking in a subconscious state.

'Krishna, come closer to me. Krishna…' the voice pleaded.

Jai sat beside the patient.

'All these years I waited for you! I thought you would come but you did not! It was entirely my fault, I…I never tried to understand you.' He said slowly between displeasing fits of cough, 'but you did not understand me either.' the voice kept on getting weaker with every word it uttered.

Jai's heart was getting heavier with every word that his ears heard. It was ready to sink beyond the deafening depths of the deepest ocean of emotions.

'You wanted to be an actor; I wanted you to become a mathematician!' Iyer's father continued.

Jai looked at the face again; suddenly it was replaced with that of his own father. He was shocked. He saw his own father confessing to him on that bed in room no 336. Now it was the turn of his eyes to sink.

The creaky voice continued, 'But I never wanted you to be a person who considered me as his enemy. I prayed that you would come back, but you did not. I would have let you do whatever you wanted to, but you never came back.'

The voice paused for a moment and then out of the silence it gleefully croaked, 'See? You are here and *Appa* did not die. Those words were powerless!' it paused again, 'I love you my son! Now do not go anywhere. Stay with me forever! Forgive this foolish old *Appa*! *Enne Mannichidu Krishna....*'

Jai stood up from the bed. He ran out of the room, tears dripping from his eyes on the way. All those words said by Iyer's father squeezed Jai's heart from all sides. He wept loudly as he ran towards the elevator. He pressed the button outside and in a minute the doors opened, he stepped inside. He quickly pressed another button and the doors closed, the elevator descended. As soon as it stopped moving, he pressed another button that opened the door. He rushed out of the lift and towards the exit as he tried hard to hide his streaming tears. The sudden emotional exchange had made him forget the fact that he was claustrophobic. He used the elevator without getting tense and breathless.

He was out of the glass building. He shouted 'Bastard! Fucking bastard! What the fuck was that fat bastard thinking when he left home! He left his fucking father to die!'

People started looking at him as he was shouting loudly.

He did not bother about those who were staring at him. He walked briskly towards the big gate through which he had got in earlier. He expected Krishnaprasad Iyer waiting with that huge tummy of his, outside the gate, waiting to know about his father and Jai was prepared to give a hard-hitting lecture to the fat man.

42

Prakash Bhawan, Gurgaon
10:30 AM

Mrs. Sharma could not take it anymore. She had waited for a long time since morning. Finally, on receiving a reluctant nod from her husband, she called the local police station and reported that her son was missing. She held the receiver close to her chest as if it contained the remnants of her *lost* son and she was not going to let it go again.

'Madam, could you please give your son's description?' The voice from the police station enquired.

Mrs. Sharma said at once, 'Tall, stout figure, with shady dark eyes. He liked to keep his hair long. Yes, it was uncut. He would wear T-Shirts over jeans. Always roamed with earphones plugged in tightly, could never leave behind his music. His complexion was fair, rather on the lighter side of fair. He is...' She was lost in his thoughts.

Silence.

'Excuse me, madam? Hello?' The voice sounded worried upon not hearing her voice for a minute.

'I am sorry, yes. He always carried his music with himself.'

'Did you contact all his friends? And their parents, his school?'

'Yes, I did. Of course, I did! His friends said that they did not know anything regarding his plans to run away. His best friend was clueless too! Otherwise, he is the one who would know everything!'

'Well, we…' there was a blinking sound in the background and then the voice continued, 'Oh! Very well, our network has shot back in. I am sorry to have kept you waiting. Kindly email your son's photo to us. We will send our men to look out for him.'

'Thank you, officer!' She said gloomily.

'We request you not to worry and keep trying from your side too. Your son will be tracked down soon. We will release his pictures on every security network spanning over the city so that we make sure we do not miss out on him at any places that are using CCTVs and centralized security networks like metro stations and certain malls and traffic signals within the city.'

'Thank you very much!'

'You are welcome madam.' The voice said and then the line went dead.

Forty-five minutes later, the phone at Prakash Bhawan rang again. A frantic Mrs. Sharma ran towards the console and picked up the receiver, she spoke in, 'Hello?' Her tone almost shrill with anxiety.

'Mrs. Sharma?' the voice enquired. She had heard the same voice some minutes ago over the same phone line.

43

Bhaktawar Singh Road, Sector 38, Gurgaon
10:50 am

Jai looked around; the road was as empty as the sound inside his heart. He looked towards his left and then scanned the periphery towards his right. He took a step forward, as he brought his neck back to the normal position.

'Where is he?' Jai asked himself. A dozen vehicles appeared on the far left side. They were heading towards Mayfield Gardens. Still far away from where Jai was standing.

Jai had expected a tense faced person to be waiting outside for him, but there was no one around except for the guards who were standing on the other side of the gate. The cars came closer and all but one of them took a right turn. The gates of the huge hospital complex opened and made way for the lush blue BMW to enter. Jai walked back to the gate, he gestured one of the guards to come. The security guard raised his eyebrow in inquisitive enquiry, '*Haan bhai?*' He asked in a native Haryanvi tone.

Jai knew the stubborn guard would not come to him. Therefore, Jai went to him instead and queried curiously, '*Jo mere saath bhai saab aaye thei, kya aapne dekha ke vo kaha gaye?*'

The dark skinned man looked at Jai and looked very irritated. He was chewing *gutka* with his roughly withered pair of lips. He spat out the chewed mixture on the tiled ground and answered, '*Tu to ekla tha... Apne aap te hi bolne laag ra tha!*'

'What? No! No! I came here with a big fat man! Almost six feet tall, huge tummy with dark skin. His name was *Iyer*. Where is he? He was waiting outside for me. Here!' he pointed at a spot just outside the gate.

'*Dekh bhai*! I too *knows the Englis*. You *cames* with *the* nobody! We *bere objerving* you at the gate, you came, you turned and you talking to yourself.' The guard cleared in his thick Haryanvi accent and broken English.

'No! I was not talking to myself, you illiterate moron! I was talking to Iyer.' He blurted in frustration.

The guard closed in on Jai. He was four inches taller than Jai and could easily feel the might of the guard superseded by a sudden gush of anger driven by his ego. '*Ke chaahve hain? Samajh na aave ke? Baawlo hai ke?* You *comes* here to tighten loose screws? *Hain?*' he threatened.

'I am not loose!' Jai was getting aggressive.

Two more guards stepped in and covered Jai from behind. Jai knew that he could not defend himself if they pounced at him. He was weaker than the weakest of the three guards. Jai retreated; he took a few steps back and turned around. He shot away as fast as he could towards the junction where Iyer and he had landed off the auto rickshaw. He ran harder as if someone had set a werewolf behind him. Nobody was following Jai, but he kept running until he reached the junction circle. Some workers were resting under a huge *peepal* tree. There was no sign of Iyer.

He saw an auto rickshaw coming his way that was going towards the Metro Station. He gestured it to halt. The three-wheeler stopped in front of him, he jumped in and they were soon moving. Jai breathed in through thick fumes of diesel that the rusty auto rickshaw emitted into the inner compartment of the three-wheeler. Jai tucked his nostrils by pulling the neck of his T-Shirt, covering his nose and entire lower facial region below it.

WHERE DID HE GO? THAT FAT BASTARD!

I KNEW HE WAS THERE, WE CAME TOGETHER.

THOSE FUCKING GUARDS MUST BE DRINKING ON DUTY.

Such thoughts kept troubling his over-stressed mind. The disappearance of Iyer was more startling than most of the events that had taken place that day including Iyer's appearance and the striking similarity between Iyer's story and his own life.

The auto rickshaw had stopped and all the passengers had got off. Jai was the last one to get off from the half-cracked metal container of a vehicle. He tipped the driver with a twenty-rupee note and ran towards the metro station. The driver called Jai to take back his change, but Jai was nowhere around to hear. He was already inside the station building.

44

Prakash Bhawan
11:15 AM

Mrs. Sharma dug into the receiver, 'Yes, did you find my son?'

'No, but we have tracked down his cellular device.' The voice replied.

'Oh Really?' She gasped in excitement.

'The device had been stationery till 12:28 am this morning. The location matches your address, which means that he had not left home until 12:28. His sim card was placed inside his cellular phone. There was movement until about two in the morning and then it was stationery till 5:30. He must have chosen to rest during this time.'

'Where?' She demanded.

'The location is somewhere near Iffco chowk. At about six, there was movement till Iffco Chowk metro station. However, within a span of twenty minutes the location changed swiftly. Finally, the phone was last recorded with the sim card intact at a place outside Ghittorni Metro Station. This is the time when he missed a call from a local number. After which we could not find either the status of the cell phone nor that of the sim card. Apparently your son did not want to be tracked down by anyone by any means, so he must have either disconnected the sim from the phone or destroyed the handset completely.'

'But why Ghittorni?'

'Well, he must have planned on using the metro till Delhi and then escape hitherto, but to his misfortunes, the metro services were temporarily closed and they were operational only until Ghittorni owing to an *accident* on the yellow line.'

'Is my son safe?'

'We all hope he is, besides, we have already sent his photo over to all the metro stations as I had mentioned earlier. We will be able to capture him soon. Keep courage and spirits high madam!'

'I am… I am' she chanted.

'I will inform you as soon as I receive any update on your son's whereabouts.'

'Thank you, Officer!'

'Goodbye!'

Mrs. Sharma placed the receiver slowly over the console. She had tears in her eyes, many beady drops of salty water. She prayed to all the gods she had heard of while growing up. She prayed hard.

45

Huda City Center Metro Station, Gurgaon
11:18 AM

Jai's eyes scanned all the corners of the station. There were more people now. The locals preferred to refer to it as the starting point for the yellow line and indeed, it was! It carried half a million people home every day. The majority bulk of them did not know that the line was temporarily suspended for the time being. On the other hand, had it been restarted? Jai barged in through the swarm of people who were on their way out of the station. All of them looked grumpy, they had hopes pinned on the metro rail for journeys to their destinations but alas! Today things were different.

Jai was looking for a man who had stormed his mind with a disillusioned story that was strikingly over whelming. He scanned everything and everyone around him to get the slightest glimpse of the man who had disappeared mysteriously. Some of the words from Iyer's story kept playing in Jai's mind. Jai was not even half the brat he was a night ago when he had decided to run away from home.

Jai walked his way to the ticket counter. Only one counter was open and it had a short queue lined up for tickets. Jai joined the queue, he was fourth. After two minutes, Jai was standing face to face with the woman who was booking tickets, just a glass interface separating them. The woman was the same one from whom he had had got his ticket in the morning. She recognized Jai's face.

The woman spoke through the interface 'You again?'

'I know that, just… just get me a ticket to Ghittorni!' Jai spoke into the interface.

'We are closing down the entire route and sir, the last train to Ghittorni leaves in 1 minute, you will not make it to the platform.'

'Will you hurry up? Here keep the change!' he said while handing over a fifty-rupee note to the woman.

She collected the money and gave him a black colored round shaped token, 'Why doesn't he use a metro card instead!'

Jai sprinted off to the security check and rushed to the platform that was two floors above from there. The train was awaiting final seconds of departure as Jai jumped into the last compartment. It was as empty as the penultimate one. The doors closed and the train moved. The journey to Ghittorni began and Jai felt that it was his last journey, the feeling of *the end* approaching surfaced out of nowhere. A bead of sweat finally appeared on Jai's forehead from beneath his long crest of black hair. The train picked up speed as it glided, screeching over the pair of metallic tracks. The image of Iyer swept through his mind along with faces formed by his imagination.

Faces straight out of Iyer's story.

46

Somewhere in New Delhi

The bus had started moving along the highway. It picked up speed fast. Hussain was seated near the rear exit. It took him fifteen minutes to arrive at the bus stop on foot. The bus was already stationed at the stop when Hussain had arrived there. The bus finally took off after another fifteen minutes, Hussain was praying. He wished to reach the lottery office before they closed down for the day. He didn't want to waste the whole day.

Hussain saw the approaching bus conductor. He slipped his hand into the pocket of his Kurta looking for his wallet. His pocket was empty, there was no wallet. He checked the other pocket anxiously. He stood up and looked around on the floor of the bus, under the seat. It was not to be seen. He ran his head trying to recollect if he had taken it out anytime. He had used a few coins to use the telephone at the metro station. He immediately informed the conductor and got off the bus. He ran towards the Metro Station. He had forgotten his wallet somewhere inside the Metro station and he was going back to get it.

This was one of the worst days of his life. But he had to do it for his sons, for little Arshad.

47

The last train arrived at the metro station on that fateful day. Jai stepped out of the train as soon as the doors pulled apart, and rode down the escalator. While he was skipping on the escalator heading downwards, constant thoughts about Iyer and his story haunted him. He saw all those things happening in front of him as he stepped on steady floor of the building from the escalator.

Jai sighed and rushed out of the room. The Café was still operational except that there was nobody inside the little *kiosk* like structure. He looked towards his left and spotted a couple of security guards standing near the entrance of the building. However, his destination was right ahead of him. Jai started walking towards it.

His heart had not been calm since Iyer had disappeared and now with every step he took towards his *destination*, the beating of the heart became mercilessly insane. Breathing became hard as he tried dragging in more oxygen with every breath he took. Blame it all on the cigarettes he had been smoking since class eleven. He exhaled swiftly leaving his respiratory tract almost devoid of rest. The air inside his body came out through his nostrils. Each step that he took towards the *destination* seemed to wrestle Jai away from it. He felt as if he was reeling backwards. He was not running yet, he was walking all right, but everything around him passed as if gravity had caught up in a web of super slow motion.

In a whisk of suspended thoughts, he was taken back to where it all began as he stood there facing the signboard that read *THE RESTING AREA*.

He pushed the door and sneaked in through the opened space. The room was empty. Jai walked towards the seat where he was sitting earlier that day. He saw the cellular phone number intact on the seat nearby. However, there was no one inside, all seats vacant. The room was as deserted as the station building itself. In the silence of the room, he could hear drops of rain pouring outside. The tickling sound made by the rain drops falling on the walls of the building paved way for a fresh set of imagery which graveled into his already preoccupied mind. His mind kept replaying the earlier events that took place in that very same room, causing further distress and arousing anxiety like never before. Three nights ago he was partying hard at a posh discotheque with his girlfriend and close friends, enjoying every moment of life as if it were his last. Two nights ago, he had broken up with his girlfriend and last night he had run away from home and now here he was rewinding everything that had happened helplessly but picturing only the fat man who had overpowered him with his story.

The eerie emptiness of the Resting Area was puncturing Jai's emotions harder than anything else that had pierced him that day, it was precisely the story he heard from the fat man whom he was looking for now.

His ears could not block away Iyer's voice; he did not even hear the sound of rain pouring outside heavily. He was standing there but his mind was in a completely different dimension.

A hand placed itself firmly on Jai's shoulder. And in that moment of crazy thoughts, everything froze. Jai's eyes popped open, silence conquered his mind and he could only hear his heart that had been pounding heavily. He inhaled a long stretch of air and slowly turned around.

This must be Iyer. He thought. This must be him. Yes, there indeed was a hand over his shoulder and as he turned around, the face of the owner revealed.

It was indeed a familiar face.

48

Jai immediately recognized that long wrinkled face. The man who still had his hand over Jai's shoulder was at least three inches taller than him. He had a neatly washed white piece of *kurta* over his upper body. He gently enquired, 'Are you looking for something?'

The Pathan's voice was the manliest baritone Jai had ever heard.

'Errr…rather *someone!* I am looking for someone.' Jai gritted.

'Someone? Who?' Hussain asked.

'Yes, of course! You were here all the time! Don't you remember that fat, middle aged man, who came in and sat next to me? The *Madrasi* guy? With a white <u>*teeka*</u>?' Jai spoke describing with the enthusiasm of a small child.

'What?' Hussain was definitely surprised.

'Yes, he kinda talked a lot, was very irritating. His name was Iyer!' Jai said.

Hussain nodded in despair and challenged Jai, 'Son, you were not sitting with anyone! Not inside this room.'

'No! His name was Iyer, Krishnaprasad Iye…'

'Son! There was no one with you. Just the two of us inside this room. I was here first and I was here even after you left this room. I saw no one except you entering and leaving the room.'

'He was sitting with me, and you saw him. You saw us talking, I know because you kept turning back now and then.' Jai screeched as he pulled the tall Pathan's collar and threateningly dragged him closer to Jai, 'His name was Iyer!'

'Are you doing *charas-ganja*? Are you taking drugs?'

'You saw us talking and you were staring at us!' Jai declared.

'*At you!* Yes! I was staring at you because of what you were doing.' Jai loosened his grip over Hussain and the tall man gently removed Jai's hands from his collar.

'What? What was I doing?' Jai asked in a meek tone.

'I heard you talking to someone, first I thought you were on the phone. However, when I turned around, I saw no phone or that thing in the ear that people wear nowadays. So, I stared at you, because you were having a conversation with yourself.'

'You are lying? Ain't you? Just like those guards, ain't you?'

'What guards?'

'Those guards at the hospital. They said they never saw anyone with me!'

'I don't know which guards you are talking about, but that is the truth. You were indeed with no one. Are you sure, you are ok?'

'Fuck you! Liars!' Jai swore loudly at Hussain.

Jai rushed out of the room. He banged the door behind him.

Hussain shook his head in shame. Slowly he reminded himself why he had come back there. He moved towards the seat where he was sitting and bent down and looked underneath.

'Aah! There it is!' He exclaimed heartily as he reached out for a torn leather wallet with his right hand.

While travelling in the bus Hussain realized that he had dropped something back in the metro station. He came back for it. He had searched the entire metro station, the phone booth and every path he had taken inside the metro station that morning. He did not find it and the one place he had not checked was the Resting Area.

When he entered the Resting Area, he found Jai standing there. The crazy boy he had encountered earlier that morning.

Young rats doing drugs. Hussain told himself as he breathed in an air of relief.

49

Control Room, Ghittorni Metro Station
12:20 noon

Jai's instincts puffed right over his intellect. He was dead sure
that he had been with the fat man. The story he told, Jai could
never have imagined all that. Maybe the Pathan was paranoid or
maybe the guards were being absent-minded while on duty and
then they were trying to hide their guilt with overt-aggression. He
had one way of finding out and he was trying to work it out.

He had gone to one of the security personnel and reported the
missing case of Iyer. Before they started scratching their heads,
Jai had tipped them to check out the surveillance cameras that
were hanging on almost every inch of the metro surroundings.
And one of them instantly assisted Jai to the control room where
everything was being monitored.

A dozen monitors mounted on the wall in front of him that
constantly flickered images after every 3 minutes displaying
every corner of the metro station and the few trains that left the
station.

'Where were you sitting?' The Security personnel asked Jai.

'We were in the Resting Area, I think at about 7:30, yea.' Jai
recollected.

The nearly emotionless Security person pressed a few keys on
the keyboard and one of the monitors drew a blank screen. Then

it showed a paused image. Jai vaguely recognized it as the Resting Area. A thunderbolt ran across Jai's face. He prayed for his belief to be right. The man pressed another button and then dragged the mouse back and forth, the image on the monitor started flickering and moving swiftly.

'7:30.' the man declared and clicked the left mouse button. The monitor slowed down and the motion stabilized.

The camera was located somewhere at the back of the room, in the right corner and mounted high upon the ceiling where nobody could touch it. Moreover, that way the camera could cover the maximum area for surveillance. There were two people sitting as it appeared on the monitor. Jai quickly recognized the man in the farther row as the Pathan and the one nearer to the camera as himself. He was wearing the same T-Shirt.

'I am going to play this at a higher speed' said the security person and then pressed a button on his keyboard. The flickering got faster but there was hardly any movement recognizable in the image. There was some neck turning from the Pathan while Jai appeared to be constantly shifting himself sideways. Though there was no sign of any third person yet. Jai had his eyes glued onto the monitor. Then the most striking thing occurred. On the monitor, he saw himself leaving the room. Much to his shock, he was moving out alone.

'Wait! Rewind and play that again, slowly.' Jai demanded.

The Security person went back by 5 minutes and played it over from there in real-time. There was no change; the same incident repeated itself, only this time it was moving slowly.

Jai felt a wall of brittle glass shattering all around him. The walls that held his sanity together now spoke in the loudest dialect ever.

'Are you sure, you were here with someone?' The man sitting with the controls asked.

Jai was mute at what he had seen on the monitor. All those

men had been right. His lips froze, he could not reply. He started walking out of the room.

'Hey! You?' The man called out from behind. Evidently, he was not very happy with Jai's reaction as the boy was starting to leave.

Jai spoke in a delusive state, 'Thank you officer. Sorry for wasting your time.' Jai apologized and shut the door slowly and started walking towards the exit at an even lesser pace. Thoughts had engulfed him from all sides.

There was no Iyer? All those people were damn right: I am crazy.

Am I in some kind of a mental shock? Is this a nightmare where I am supposed to wake up and find myself in my bed? Oh God! Let it be that way.

I cannot take this anymore.

I wish I were back home with my mother.

With my father.

All those characters from Iyer's story appeared in front of him as he walked in the direction of the building's exit.

Excuse me? Can I sit here?

These seats are all dirty, it will spoil my waisty'

The Greatest epic is your own life's story.

Would you do me a favor?

I don't know you or your name, but I would like to give you one small piece of advice.'

Jai's mind kept zigzagging through various conversations he had with Iyer.

'So, I shouldn't have run away?'

'What would you do if you were in my place?'

All the thoughts faded away into one single thought that now bound Jai's conscience solidly.

I AM IN HIS PLACE.

A tear jerked off his eye. In a moment of confusion he realized the righteous truth that he was about to commit the greatest mistake of his life.

Besides the recap of everything, he was also getting that weird nauseating urge to throw up. Things were spinning around him. The motion was certainly circular. He was going down.

While walking out of the station someone grabbed him from behind. The action took Jai by shock and he instantly fainted and passed out.

50

Ghittorni Metro Station
Twenty minutes ago

'Sir, this is Lieutenant Rajbir Singh Ranawat, reporting from the control room, Ghittorni Metro Station.' The tall security person said into the mobile phone.

After a slight delay a voice replied from the other end of the line 'Inspector Vijay Pratap here.'

'I wish to report the sighting of a young boy who is presumed missing since yesterday. We had his image fed into our database this morning itself.'

'Oh! Wait, is it…' the inspector paused to recollect and then spoke, 'is it the tall teenager, fair in complexion. His name… Jai Prakash Sharma?'

'Yes, tall with long dark hair. Wearing a T-shirt and baggy jeans.'

'Where is he?'

'He was here in the morning; I remembered his face because there were not many people who came here because of the accident.'

'What time?'

'He was here early and left after some time.'

'Why? Why didn't you stop him?' The inspector charged.

'Inspector, we had received the update on our database, just half an hour ago. It was not written on his face, you see.' The Security person thwarted.

The inspector sighed.

'But he came back a minute ago and he is heading towards the Resting Area once again, where he had been this morning. I think he's going to hide there.' Rajbir slipped in.

It brought fresh hope in the voice of the inspector and he said, 'Look! Do not pounce on him. Be gentle and keep an eye on him as long as he is there, make sure that he does not leave the station building anytime soon, if he does then follow him. Do not take him under custody unless he is boarding some vehicle. Do you get me?'

'I get that. You want me to prey silently, keep vigil?'

'Exactly! You know these new generation kids get grapy easily. That is the first place why he is wandering like this. He has given his parents a tough time, especially his mother. You stick around and keep me updated. I will be there with my men in fifteen minutes.'

'Sure.' Lieutenant Rajbir Singh said and then hung up the phone. He knew he had to be patient with the boy until the cops arrived.

Hardly ten minutes later, the boy himself came to Rajbir Singh. He carried a worried look on his handsome face. He told the security personnel about a mysterious, fat man and asked him if they could check out the CCTV recordings from the morning. Rajbir had to agree because that way he could keep the boy around for a little longer until the cops dashed in.

He had agreed.

51

Hussain although perturbed had put on a consolidating smile on his face as he neared his little shelter. He could see his young ones playing outside while the eldest one was still pouring milk into the over used kettle placed neatly on the little kerosene stove. He saw his father approaching and immediately his worn out face was lit up with a sparkling smile. A smile that carried the zeal of hope and promises. He greeted his father. Hussain could smile in the darkest of hours, such a way had he been shaped since childhood; this wasn't the worst of what he had seen in his life. He smiled and he greeted back Arshad.

Hussain walked into his little hut. His wife was packing some used clothes into a cardboard box; she immediately identified the arrival of her husband.

'You have arrived. I shall make something, please give me a moment. My mistress,' she explained while pushing the box neatly under a shackled table, 'Mrs. Ahuja gave some of their children's old woollens. It was so kind of her. *Allah* bless her kind soul. Now we don't have to worry about the kids this winter. You can think about purchasing the mobile phone. It has become a necessity nowadays for everyone."

For a moment Hussain thought about the arrogant teenager

he had met at the metro station. It was quite strange that he didn't carry any mobile phone. Maybe he didn't flash it like others his age do. Most the time these brats carried two or three big sized phones.

"What are you thinking about?" His wife enquired.

Hussain passed the question and began undressing his Kurta.

"How did it go at the Lottery office?" She asked.

Hussain sighed.

"I couldn't make it to the Lottery office today. A mishap occurred on the metro line. Some poor being lost his life, may *Allah* grant peace to his soul." Hussain explained.

His wife had a sudden look of anxiety on her face, "Is everything alright?"

"It's a long story. After waiting for the metro line to open at the station I decided to take a bus to Delhi. While on the bus I realized I had lost my wallet which contained money as well as the ticket somewhere at the metro station. I had to go back. The lottery office was closing down early today. I couldn't make it in time, so I came back."

"What are we going to do now?" Her eyes started filling up.

"Nevertheless, I called up the Lottery office before they closed. One has a deadline of an entire week; the winning candidate must appear within the week of declaration. We didn't have to hurry. I shall leave early in the morning tomorrow."

He paused to look at his wife. She was already sulking mildly. He put his arm around her shoulder and pulled her towards him, close. He wiped her tear and assured, "Everything is going to be alright. Everything is *Allah's* will. Keep faith."

She surrendered unto her husband's faith and closed her eyes as she placed her head gently on his bare chest.

"Do you think our son is happy here?" Hussain asked.

Hussain's wife couldn't place the context for such a question. She nodded, "Why do you ask such a question?"

"Kids his age go to school, play around. Not just that we cannot afford to send him to school. We can and will be sending the young ones to school someday but Arshad will be grown up by then. He has been shouldered with so much responsibility already. *His dreams will go unseen in the light of our expectations.*"

"His only dream is to keep his *Abbu* happy."

"How can you be so sure?" Hussain's eyes were diluted as well. His eyes had filled up only once before and that was long ago when he was a little boy and was left alone to die in a railway yard as his family abandoned him. He had never taken to tears again since then.

"I'm his mother. I can tell. Keep faith in *Allah*." She gave an assuring smile.

"*Abbu*," a voice said from behind, it was Arshad. He was holding a few currency notes in hand, "everyone liked our tea today Abbu. Everyone was happy. Here is the money, lot of money. We can buy a teastall near the ma... maa..."

"Mall" Hussain filled in.

"Yes, Abbu. If we keep selling good tea everyday like this, we will have more happy customers and soon we can start it." The little boy said innocently.

Hussain released his wife and turned towards his son and gently lifted him up in the air, holding him tightly, "You are a little man... having a modest dream... but a big heart!"

Arshad chuckled joyfully. He hardly understood what his father said but he knew he was being complimented and he loved it. Hussain's other kids joined the scene playfully. They all shared the little joys of life. Hussain was happy that his son wasn't like that arrogant teenager at the metro station.

Allah had indeed blessed him.

52

Prakash Bhawan
05:53 PM

There was a slight strain in the forehead. Jai felt something pushing his eyebrow inwards but that did not stop him from looking around. There were people. Lots of them and somebody shouted out something in excitement.

Jai realized he was lying down on something. Something soft. He had been on that *something* before, many times earlier. He felt that familiar softness on which he had been resting his body for the past three years. It was his own bed.

Then a woman appeared from somewhere in his view, with tears in her eyes. She carried a plumbing smile and instinctively thanked God, '*Hey Ram! Tera laakh laakh Shukar hai!*'

'Mom? What has happened?' Jai gargled in a hush voice.

The woman pressed on the boy who was lying on the bed. Jai was happy to see his mother who could not hold her tears but he still could not place himself in that situation. What had happened?

'Hey bro!' a very familiar voice called out.

Jai turned towards another figure. Anwar was standing there with a warm hand on Jai's naked shoulder.

'*Yaar!* You're here! Where is...' Jai tried hard but he could not speak more.

'*Sab theek hai.* Everything is all right.' Anwar guaranteed.

'*Woh?*' Jai asked.

'*Woh bhi.* She's at her grandma's in Simla. She has sent her warmest wishes.'

'My head is spinning, I don't understand anything.' Jai confessed.

'Hey bro! chill, Everything's cool! We all love you!' He smiled and pressed Jai's palm gently with his.

Jai smiled. He looked around. Last thing that came into his mind was a fat man and his piercingly luring story. According to his mind, He was not supposed to be where he was right now. He could not gauge what had happened. Hadn't he run away from home? Shouldn't he have caught a train to Mumbai? There was confusion and a corrosive headache.

And before Jai could think further a fifty something man appeared and sat on the bed, next to Jai. He gently ran his hand through Jai's long hair. He used to hate the young boy's hair, rather their length. He would always demand a reduction in length. However, today he loved everything about his son.

'Dad? Oh! Dad. I do not understand anything. I thought... I thought I was...' Jai tried to recollect.

'It was just a bad dream, son. Just a bad dream.' The mathematician caressed his son.

'But why are there so many people here? Dad!' Jai cried.

'Last night you ran a very high fever and then you passed out due to the fever. We all thought we would lose you, so your friends came to see you. We were all praying, son!'

'But... but... the letter! My letter, did you read that?'

'What letter?' Mr. Sharma asked inadvertently.

'The l...' Jai paused and sighed, 'Never mind!'

'How are you feeling now?'

'I am sorry Dad! I am extremely sorry. I am young and I agree I am an idiot. I will do whatever you ask me to do.'

'Really?' His father rechecked.

Jai wanted to take his words back, but then he decided against it, 'Yes, Dad! I will do *whatever* you ask me to.'

'I want you to,' Mr. Sharma smiled gently and continued, 'I want you to take rest and get well soon. I love you son! Now go to sleep, we will wake you up for dinner later.'

Jai smiled back. He did not want his father to leave. Somehow, he wanted to rest his tired head on his father's lap, as he used to do as a 9 year old. However, some unfamiliar names and faces kept hanging around his head. It all felt very strange and heavy. But like his father had said, it was *just a bad dream*. Maybe he had encountered a ghost or it was just a part of his conscience that took the form of a fat man and made him realize that he had to go back home. That he had to go back to his father before he would lose him and everything forever. What was his name again? The fat man who narrated a story in Jai's *dream.*

Jai felt a slight prick in his buttock. Soon he felt drowsy and it was time to dream again. Meet that man again, maybe.

Iyer, Krishnaprasad Iyer.

53

May 22, 2010
06:15 PM

'Thank you very much children.' Mr. Sharma announced gratefully.

'It's always cool, *uncleji,* we all love Jai as much as you do!' Anwar clarified.

'Please make sure that nobody ever reveals what had happened to Jai. *Ever!*' Sharma warned.

'We will make sure of that, *uncleji.*'

'If he asks, just tell them, it was a dream. *He never ran away from here,* there was no letter. You simply cover up with the story that I made up, ok?'

'Of course, now if you may, we gotta go. It is late.'

'Thank you, *beta.* Sure, you must leave for your parents will be waiting for you too. We need to have a quiet family dinner with our son.' Mr. Sharma finally said.

The teenagers left and Mrs. Sharma locked the door. She looked at her husband who was just standing next to her. She was not crying anymore.

'Why did you lie to Jai?' She demanded.

'I just did not want to remind him of something that would make him run away again.'

'But I thought that you did not care. You said he was a

weakling, you were so harsh on him this morning.' She accused her husband.

'He is a weakling, definitely. My measurements are never wrong.'

'Then? Why is this sudden change of mind? What may have caused it?'

'A mathematical equation. Rather a proposition.' He said.

'What?' Mrs. Sharma was surprised to hear that.

'Well, it goes like this, Priya, *X is directly proportional to Y*, where X is the anger and frustration of a father.'

'And Y?'

'The love and care of a father. You see, he might be a weakling, and that too a pathetic one, but at the end of the day, he is my only son and I love him more than anything in this world. Even the numbers that I am so proud of are just so infinitesimally smaller than the love for my son.'

'Awww!' the wrinkled face of the wife had the tears in her eyes and she quickly pressed herself on her husband's aged but strong shoulders.

'Priya, Back in my college days, one of my hostel mates made me watch a *South Indian* movie. I understood most of the movie because there were subtitles for those who did not understand his language. There was one line that stayed with me forever.'

'What was that?'

'*The earth revolved around the sun and the universe revolved around MATHEMATICS!* I liked that very much, touched me. But today, I realized something.'

'And…?' She waited for him to reveal.

'Mathematics might be the greatest force. So great, that the earth and the universe may be circling it. But it is still incompetent because there is no number in mathematics which could measure the amount of love I have in my heart for my son.'

The woman did not know what to say. She simply clang to the man's chest.

'The police did not find Jai's cell phone. What are we going to tell him when he asks about it?' She asked concernedly.

'Tell him that *you lost it somewhere.*' Mr. Sharma suggested.

'Why is it always I who has to take responsibility?'

'Come on! I will be the one who will be buying him a new iPhone, so you take the little blame. He will get over Nokia soon.'

She held her husband tightly for another moment before they finally went their ways. She went to the kitchen and he went to wake Jai up for dinner.

54

Next day, May 23, 2011
10:25 AM

The morning was splendid. Jai woke up early, which in itself was a wondrous event. His father had never witnessed such a phenomenon ever before. This was surely a positive change in Jai.

Mr. Sharma was all smiles. After having a quick breakfast and bidding goodbye to his rushing father, Jai sat down on the couch in front of him. He felt different because nobody talked about higher studies or asked *'what are you going to do next?'* kind of questions at the breakfast table that morning. His father's plan had worked pretty well and Jai was convinced that he was unconscious and all that had happened was just a dream he had had while he was unconscious. He picked up the morning newspaper. He unfolded the front sheet; his head still had a strange dizziness around it.

He concentrated on the newspaper. The first news on the front page had a huge picture of tall black man with long hair. He read the headline-

Gayle storms Superkings, helps Bangalore win by 8 wickets
Superkings? Somebody told me he liked Superkings. Who was that? Jai thought.

He liked the Daredevils but unfortunately Delhi was still placed at the bottom in the year's League table. Therefore, the event that was rocking the entire country did not stir Jai even by an ounce of a bit. He moved onto the next headline.

Miraculous surgery saves 67 year old man

A small photo of the man who had survived the miracle placed at the center of the news piece drew a very familiar picture. Jai had seen this man before.

But Where?

The question bugged him. He had seen that man somewhere, and that too very recently. All this aggravated his headache. He closed in on the details. There was a mention of a *Dr. Jaydev Singh*. The name was familiar too. However, before he could read further, another news headline caught his attention.

Man crushed to death; halts Gurgaon Metro Line for 11 hours

Jai started reading that particular news. He ran through the first few lines quickly and then slowed down with every detail that he got. Every word he read caused his heart to pump blood faster. Some person had been run over by a Gurgaon Metro Bombardier train on it is journey towards *Huda City Center*. Apparently, the man was standing with his back resting on the door. The door opened accidentally while the train was in full motion. He fell off the train into the other track and was run over by another train that was heading towards Jahangirpuri. There were some words that were highlighted with vague familiarities- *Gurgaon Metro, Yellow line halted, Ghittorni, bulky man* etc. Jai recollected the entire *dream* he had last night. All those names and nouns had a special mention in his dream. He knew he was close to something and absolutely believed the possibility that it all had happened to him yesterday. Tension grew within him as he read on.

The next paragraph contained the description of the victim's identity. He was identified as a 30 something man of Tamil origin. Jai was about to read the next line which would reveal the name of the person and then his doorbell rang. The sudden outburst of cuckoo's call shook Jai.

There was absolute silence.

Jai stood up slowly and then walked to the door. His heart had already lost faith in his body. Cautiously he turned the knob of the door and opened it.

55

There was a tall man standing in front of Jai. His wrinkled face had the clear resemblance of somebody whom Jai had seen in his *dream*. He had had a conversation with the person in that *dream*. Now, that man was there right in front of Jai. The man himself had a very tense expression on his face. He was panting in halves.

Everything in the *dream* was recurring in his real life. The man who survived the surgery, the name of the surgeon, the train accident and *the metro station*. The dream was too real to be false or was it really a dream? Jai started losing his mind as confusion crept in.

He looked into the eyes of the tall man and enquired, 'You?' The question was rather a conformational enquiry. Jai was trying to confirm that he had indeed met him a day ago. He asked 'I... I know you!'

'Yes, *Salaam Vaalekhum!*' the tall Pathan greeted.

Jai nodded blankly.

'I am glad that you remember me from our brief encounters from yesterday' The Pathan acknowledged.

'So, we did meet. It was real.'

'Yes, I am sorry. I am Hussain Ansari. I own a small tea stall in Ghittorni.'

'Ok, what are you doing here? How did you find me?' Jai thought for a moment and then accused, 'Are you following me?'

'No! No! Son, I am not following you. I just wanted to return something.'

'Return what?'

Hussain threw his left hand into the *kurta's* pocket, produced a gadget, and said showing it to Jai, 'I think this belongs to you.'

Jai looked at the gadget, it was a Nokia mobile phone wrapped in its earphone. He identified immediately it as the phone, which he owned. The phone that he had had thrown away in his *dream*, a dream that did not seem like a dream anymore. He took it from Hussain's withered hand.

'Where did you find it? And how did you know it belonged to me? Did you see me throwing it away?'

'No! Of course not'

'Then? Please tell me, and how the hell did you find out where I live?' Jai looked at the man's beard and other facial features and asked accusingly, 'Are you a *mujahidin* or something? Were you tracking me down? Did you plant something in my phone?'

'No! No!'

'Then how do you explain everything? Or am I *dreaming* again?'

'No, you are not dreaming. You are not crazy either.'

'What do you mean?' Jai asked.

'I am sorry but yesterday I seriously suspected that you were crazy. You were either talking to yourself or talking total non-sense. I was sure you were crazy,' Hussain came closer and whispered, 'but now I know you are not crazy. *It is real*, it is true!'

'What is true? Tell me, what is real?'

Hussain fell silent for a moment and then spoke three words in a tone that punctured silence out of the air, '*He was there!*'

56

Metro Station Platform, Ghittorni
Few hours ago

It was early in the morning and Hussain stood on the platform along with a bunch of other commuters eagerly waiting for the first train for Jahangirpuri to arrive. Once again, He had left all the duties of the tea stall to his eldest son, Arshad. Hussain had clear intentions: he would go to the Lottery office, fill up all the forms and get the money as soon as possible. He had already wasted a day. Hussain had forgotten about his encounter with the crazy boy who talked to himself. The previous day he had to return home in disappointment because he couldn't make it to the Lottery office in time. He was allowed one chance. His wife and son Arshad were supportive, they did not complain.

He kept gazing at the railway track ahead. There was no sign of the arriving train. Tired, he decided to sit down on the bench lying three steps behind him. He placed himself on the bench: there was space for one more person to sit. Hussain kept his carry bag there, right next to him on the seat.

The air went cold all of a sudden and Hussain started shivering from the sudden chill. He wondered if anyone else around him felt the chill.

'*Excuse me? Can I sit here*' asked someone. A chilled breeze shot through him.

Hussain did not look at the person. He felt that it was his duty to let the person sit regardless of who or what he was. Hussain picked up his carry bag and placed it on the floor below, between his two legs. The person sat down; there was a mild *thud* as he sat on the metallic seat. The man was *bulky*.

'My Name is *Iyer, Krishnaprasad Iyer.*' The fat man introduced himself as he held out his thick brown hand for a shake.

The name rang a deafening bell in Hussain's head, it sounded very recent.

Yes, of course, he had heard that name just a day ago. The cold air sent a chill of terror down Hussain's spine. His eyes opened wide in shock. He doubted whether he had also started hearing and seeing things like the boy whom he had called crazy a day ago. Had his mind also started playing tricks with him? Gathering a few ounces of courage and resilience, Hussain turned towards the fat man. He was dark, bulky and funny looking with a stroke of *vibhuti* on his forehead: just as the boy had described.

'H...how may I help you?' Hussain trembled as he asked, more because of fear.

'Will you do me a favor?' Iyer asked.

'What favor?'

Iyer produced a Nokia cellular phone and an earphone cord wound around it like a serpent around the trunk of a sandal tree.

'Could you please deliver this to its owner? He must be worried.' Iyer requested.

'But... but... Whose phone is it?'

'A little friend whom I met yesterday. Young and full of energy.'

'Was he tall and fair with long hair?'

'Aaah! You seem to know him too!' Iyer exclaimed, 'so, it will be easier for you to find him. You were there at the resting hall as well.' He smiled at the shivering Pathan.

The sound of the approaching train was heard from a distance. There was movement on the platform. People were getting ready.

'But where do I go? Besides, I am in a hurry right now. I have to…'

'You finish your own work first. You can deliver this on your way back. The address is written on this paper. Please, I would be very grateful to you.' He said as he handed a crumpled piece of paper to Hussain.

'Are you sure this is the correct address?' Hussain confirmed.

'I found it written on the battery of the phone with a white correction pen. I wrote it down in this piece of paper. Maybe his father is a wise man: he must have been apprehensive that his son might lose the cell phone and took this precaution. He trusted that the person who found it would return it too.'

'But why don't you give it?' Hussain asked amidst the noise of the approaching train.

'I am running out of time, my dear brother! *I am running out of time.* I have to go back to where I came from. *Where we all come from.*'

The train entered the platform now, and it blew a deafening whistle as it applied brakes. The sound caught Hussain's attention: he turned to look at the train. However, when he turned back, the fat man was gone and so was the chilly feeling.

The train had pulled over coming to a complete stop. Hussain rose from the seat, picked up his carry bag from the floor, and walked slowly into the train.

As the train started moving, Hussain realized that the boy he had met yesterday was not lying nor was he a lunatic. There was indeed a man called Iyer and today he had shown himself to Hussain. He knew that nobody else had seen the fat man. Nevertheless, he was in a hurry today. '*I am running out of time.*' He had told Hussain. Was he going back to heaven? Hussain closed his eyes and prayed to the almighty, to *Allah*. After all, he had seen a dead man today, *a ghost*!

Epilogue

Three years later
May 22, 2014
Delhi

People would laugh at me when I told them that I had once been with a ghost. Nobody believed me and before they could label me as a mad man, I would break out into sadistic laughter: putting an end to their suspicions and proverbial deductions. They would infer that I had a terrific sense of humor. Indeed, I did.

However, I shall always savor the truth, which was itself partly revealed. A highly effervescent truth: proof of which did not exist.

Sometimes, I would ponder upon the events that took place on that day, May 22 of 2011. The big fight with my father, running away from home and especially my encounter with Iyer and his story. The story that was scripted as a cautionary tale for me so I could reconsider the course of life I was gonna take. The junky guy from Chennai could gleefully get into a conversation with just anyone. Life had shaped him that way. While his story shaped my life into a fruitful validation, I never saw Iyer again. He had disappeared.

There were moments that made me reconsider my decision and the most important among them was the one where I had a tryst with Iyer's dad in the hospital room. It was not Iyer's dad whom I saw there, lying on that bed; *I saw my own dad*, in that position. I realized that I was doing the same thing, taking Iyer's position in a story that had me in the lead.

Back home, my father made me believe that I had a *bad dream*. I believed him, though later truth resurfaced. The man, who had called me crazy earlier, ended up at my door, in an effort to return my phone. He had also seen the ghost. The ghost who had sent my cellular phone through him. I did see that man again after six months in a new mall in Gurgaon. He runs a popular cafe with his young son. I occasionally visited the place. He serves the best tea in the world, very reasonably priced and tastes of heaven. Validates the name of his shop, 'Jannat'. We talk a lot whenever I go there. A wonderful human being and his young son inspires me with his determination.

The first time I visited the place, the Pathan immediately recognized me. He told me what Iyer had told him that day.

I am running out of time, my dear brother! I am running out of time. I have to go back to where I came from. Where we all come from.

Those were his departing words. I wondered what language they spoke in *that place*. Tamil would have been comfortable for him.

My father still tells me that I never ran away. I just nod in agreement.

I had told him that I would never be a successful engineer; nevertheless, I would still do whatever he wanted me to do. But, he no longer wanted me to be an engineer. He had left it up to me. Therefore, I did what I had planned for, Animation.

This morning (on this very day of May 22) I got a call from a huge multimedia company based in *Chennai*. Every man in the industry wants to work there.

Soon, I will be leaving for Chennai, the city where Iyer had lived half of his life. The city that Iyer had praised and cursed so much in his story.

Coincidence?

Maybe I will start learning Tamil and audition for a few Tamil action flicks, couldn't I? (If Hindi speaking girls can be heroines in Tamil movies, why can't there be a hero from the North?)

My parents are very happy for me. My father really appreciates the efforts that I have put in to reach thus far.

I learnt to ignore *overreacting*, something I should have done a long time back. Ignore things that provoke you, instead of reacting to them. Laugh your way through everything, everyday. It is funny but at the end of the day, we are all dirt in the sand. What is the point in wiping off the dirt, when you know you will be covered again soon?

And of course, we made up after I came back home, *Tania and I*. We have been together since then. She completes me and I hope to get married to her in a year or two.

The Resting Area in that Metro Station was closed down two years ago. Since no other Metro Station had such a facility, the metro authority felt that an *extra room* accessible to the public was not required anymore. But little does anyone know the significance of that extra room, except for me.

Now, after all this I feel like writing down my entire experience. Like in a novel or an autobiography. Maybe a novel? What name shall I use as the title for such a novel?

My Name is Iyer can be a good title, but sounds like a spoof on the Bollywood film, *My Name is Khan*. No Sir, I don't *wanna* get into any *kinda* legal mess.

The man who came sounds quite okay too.

I could also use *Running Away* as the title of my novel.

Naah! All these titles seem vaguely out of context. I know what the most appropriate title for my novel would be.

The perfect name, the perfect noun.

A title that justifies the entire story.

The title that is directly linked to the soul of the story.

The moment when the runaway came face to face with the man who came. The moment …

"WHEN STRANGERS MEET.."

Jai Prakash Sharma
May 22, 2014, Gurgaon

News Paper Report

Man crushed to death; halts Gurgaon Metro Line for 11 hours
By: Devendra Kumar, Gurgaon express
May 22, 2011

A man in his 30s was killed after falling off a Gurgaon metro train by another metro which was approaching from the opposite side ran over him near Ghittorni, Delhi on Saturday night.

The Police say just before 11 pm on Saturday, they received a call that a man had been run over by a Metro train on the Yellow line of Gurgaon Metro.

Inspector Ramnik Kaul said that no foul play was suspected. Neither was the victim under the influence of alcohol. The victim was standing near the door with his back resting on the door of the moving train. The door opened accidentally while moving and he fell off the train. Another train was coming from the opposite direction on the parallel track, which ran over the middle-aged man.

Mallika Yadav, spokesperson for *Delhi Metro*, told Gurgaon Express that the incident is a tragic reminder that people should listen and follow the cautionary rules that are constantly announced inside the metro trains, 'Do not stand at the door.'

Yadav said that one of the track surveyors noticed the man lying on the track early in the morning. He was already dead.

'It's an unfortunate accident which could have been avoided. It is an opportunity for a safety reminder that people should use extreme caution. This sort of carelessness can lead to tragic consequences. It's very sad." She addressed the media.

Meanwhile Inspector Kaul revealed that the primary investigation by the police had been completed. They had found a wallet in the pocket of his shirt. The man was identified as Krishnaprasad Iyer, a resident of Chennai working for the Chennai Municipal Corporation. Details about his family are being tracked by the police. Till now nobody has come to claim his body.

Acknowledgement

For the stories she would read to me on hazy afternoons in the 90's, my heartiest gratitude goes out to Mahalakshmi Krishnamoorthy, my mother.

To Shri Krishnamoorthy P, my father, for being the hero... the greatest inspiration for this story... To Kunyappa & Kunyaapi...

The journey of Iyer began with my first attempt at making films. I'd thank Varun & Abhimanyu for supporting me at that time. Jashandeep for his Haryanvi input. Sakshi Garg for contributing such beautiful illustrations. Mrs. Anju Joshi, R.Sudarsan & Dr. Patro for motivating me to keep on rowing at those times when I feared my ship would sink. Venu Uncle & Rema Aunty for their warm hospitality.

Writers Dan Brown & Paulo Coelho, for the influence of their works on me has been profound.

Last but perhaps the most, my publisher Mr. Bose for agreeing to publish my work.

To Our Parents... Our God...

Srishti's all time bestsellers ₹ 100 each

- A Dilli-Mumbai Love Story
- A Feeling Beyond Words
- A half baked love story
- A Little Bit of Love...
- A Little Love Incident
- And then it rained....
- A Roller Coaster Ride!
- As Long as I Love you...
- A thing beyond forever
- Because you Loved me..
- Beep you! you BeepHole
- Boundless Saga of Love
- Can't Cook a Love Story
- Corporate Atyaachaar
- Crazy Bloody Thing LOV
- Everything you Desire
- Few things left unsaid
- Heartbreaks & Dreams!
- I am Broke....! Love me
- I am Still Committed..
- If God went to B-School
- If I Pretend I am Sorry!
- It Happened that Night
- In Course of True Love
- It's all About Love...
- It Should Be u!! My Love

- It wasn't Love at First
- Jab se you have loved me
- Journey of two Hearts
- Life is What you Make it
- Love Happens Like that
- Love, Life & A Beer Can!
- Love, me and Bullshit!
- Love Power Politics!!
- Love a Rather Bad Idea
- LUV is a Dirty Business
- Nothing Lasts Forever
- Of Tattoos and Taboos!
- Oops! 'I' fell in Love!
- Ouch! that 'Hearts'..
- Patyala Down De Throat
- Plz.. Kiss me or Kill me
- She is Single I'm Taken
- 34 Bubblegums and Candies
- That Kiss in the Rain..
- The Idiot-Dudes.....
- The India I Dream of
- The Lost Scraps of Love
- The Off-Site Tamasha
- The Quest for Nothing!
- The Thing Between U & Me
- Those Small Lil Things

- Brain Building for achievement
- Cheiro's : Language of the Hand

- Winning Personality: